IN THE SHADOW OF

PORTER'S HOLLOW

Yvonne Schuchart

ISBN 13: 978-1-942430-86-5
ISBN 10: 1-942430-86-8

Year of the Book
135 Glen Avenue
Glen Rock, PA 17327

Library of Congress Control Number: 2016951991

DEDICATION

This book is dedicated to you, dear reader.

Your time is precious to me.

ACKNOWLEDGMENTS

I want to thank my fiancè, Earl, for believing in me and encouraging me to keep writing. Without his cheerleading voice telling me I could do this, I'm not sure I would have had the fortitude to stick it out to the finish.

My multi-talented and lovely daughter Rebecca Magar deserves highest accolades. She created the amazing cover for this book. She also hosts my website and gives me constant technical advice, especially with social media. Her talents include website hosting, freelance artist and graphic design. Look her up at wailingwizard.com or @FantasyArtRebecca for her artwork and www.spasticghost.com for web hosting services.

Thank you to my other children: Kimberly Albert, Aaron Zimmerman and Amy Zimmerman and their families who encouraged and supported me all along. I especially thank each of you for your loving patience when I didn't have time for you because I was writing.

A big thanks to everyone in my writer's groups for their helpful comments, tips and proofreading. Again, I couldn't have done this without all of you behind me.

Lastly, I have to thank Demi Stevens of Year of the Book press for—well—everything! You've taught me so much. You helped me sculpt my work with care, and inspired me to believe in myself.

". . . one can never leave home . . . one carries the shadows, the dreams, the dragons of home under one's skin, at the extreme corners of one's eyes . . ."

–Maya Angelou, *Letter to My Daughter,* 2008

PROLOGUE

ROBERTA FOSTER

"Superstitions are, for the most part, but the shadows of great truths."
~Tryon Edwards, *A Dictionary of Thoughts*, 1897.

Thursday, September 1, 1960

Roberta Foster shivered as she stepped out of the local doctor's house on the night of that first disappearance. There was an unnatural frostiness to the air. She pulled her sweater tight, turned up the dirt road toward home—and stopped short. A barred owl hooted from a fork in the tree above her. Goosebumps raised the hairs on her arms. It was the third time in a week she'd heard that call. According to mountain folks, when you hear an owl hoot three times, death is coming for someone.

It was a long, solitary walk back over the mountain through Porter's Hollow. She scanned the inky woods and the road ahead. The moon shone big and bright, deepening the shadows along the path. Lord knows she had enough to think on, but it was hard to concentrate on such a night.

Robey was in quite a fix. She was in love with a local boy, Glen Allen Porter. He was tall and muscular, with dark hair, fair skin and soft grey eyes. And he understood how bad she wanted to get away from here. Kept telling Robey how much he loved her even though he went and married that . . . well, she was too much of a lady even to think the word.

Still, she should've been more careful. She knew better 'cause her own mother had done the same. But her momma hadn't lived long enough to raise her.

Aunt Hattie had taken her in when Momma died and she never asked anything. They lived in a white-washed, two-story clapboard on a few acres Hattie Perkins' husband left her when he passed. But they weren't well off, and they had no car so they walked pretty much everywhere. Which was why Robey found herself out on the road alone so late at night. The Doc saw her in his home after work for nothing more than a few dozen eggs, and some tobacco now and then.

She generally didn't mind walking, but this felt like a hair-raising, bone-chilling sort of night. All the same, Robey admired the silvery glow of the moon—right up until she spotted something white floating above the road straight ahead.

She shuddered as a tingle crawled up her spine and spread to cover her scalp. Robey drew her sweater close and cradled her swollen belly in both arms. The specter appeared to glide along the ground toward her. She caught her breath and froze. It glowed ghostly pale in the moonlight as it stopped just out of arm's reach. Then it shook itself all over and sat down to look at her.

"Oh, Heaven's sake, it's just a puppy," she chided on a rush of exhaled breath. It comforted Robey to talk to her unborn child, made her feel like she wasn't alone in the eerie night.

The ghostly mutt sat there and stared at her, head cocked. It whined and dropped to the ground, chin on its paws. Then it stood back up, shook itself again and trotted off across the road. But it stopped on the other side and turned to look back at her once more.

Robey sighed, "I know I shouldn't follow that thing." Yet after a moment's hesitation, she made to move toward it. She gave a light whistle and called, "Here boy, c'mon now, we won't hurtcha."

The little beast blinked and turned away. It scampered through the gully and down the pasture edge by the roadside where it scuttled under a fence. What happened next made Robey's limbs go heavy and drained the blood from her face.

The ghostly pale creature passed under the wooden fence rail—and disappeared.

Robey stepped forward searching despite her fearful superstitions. She peered hard into the darkness as she bent down and felt the rail, the ground under it, the air around it, but there was no sign of the animal. And no bushes or groundhog holes for it to hide in. No explanation for its disappearance.

A moment later, Robey heard a high-pitched, agonized scream from somewhere not far up the hollow. She stood so abrupt-like she stumbled and fell backward. Landed so hard on her bottom on the graveled roadside, it drove the breath right out of her. Hands scraped stones as she attempted too late to catch herself.

In that same instant she felt a pop as a rush of warm fluid gushed out from between her legs. A sharp cry of fear and pain escaped her own mouth. Roberta Foster wasn't sure what she'd heard at the time. It all fused into one overwhelming experience as she went into labor, her sense of anxious dread almost as intense as the pain.

Yet a short few hours later, she delivered a normal, healthy baby girl.

But the disappearing little white dog had surely been an omen. Because, as Robey found out later, something unspeakable happened to someone else small, pale and defenseless that night. Something that would cast a long dark shadow over her own little girl's life forever.

CHAPTER 1

LAURA EVANS

Tuesday, August 3, 2010

Laura Evans sat in the front center chair, hands folded in her lap, staring straight ahead as she watched the clear sparkling droplets gather undisturbed on a silver-grey casket. The weather was supposed to be clear so they hadn't set up a tent. Yet it wasn't raining exactly, just misting heavily, like the sky was weeping.

Doug wouldn't have wanted a tent anyway. He loved the outdoors, they both did.

Without a sound, she drew a deep breath, then exhaled slow and quiet. She sat motionless while the minister's voice droned on.

Twenty-seven years of Laura's life lay in a smooth, metallic-silver coffin, ready to be put in the ground forever. But tears wouldn't come. They crowded inside her head and heart along with everything else she'd lost and couldn't let go of. *Emotional death*. She'd heard the term somewhere before.

Laura turned her head and caught her mother's gaze. Roberta Foster Maitlin had been through this herself a few years ago. She'd been dry-eyed then, and she was dry-eyed now.

The minister's voice cut into her thoughts, "To everything there is a season and a time to every purpose under the heaven: A time to be born, and a time to die; a time to plant, and a time to pluck up that which is planted; a time to kill, and a time to heal; a time to break down . . ." *A time to break down*. Laura thought about her last real conversation with Doug. He'd come home late again and went straight to his den. "Paperwork," he mumbled as he passed her in the hall.

At the dinner table later, he barely looked up as he read the news. Laura made an attempt at conversation. "I'm leaving for Italy tomorrow," she declared.

"Hmm? Oh, yeah?" he mumbled.

"Yeah, think I'll do a month-long wine country tour. Go to Rome, Venice. It'll be fun to go alone," Laura watched his face waiting for some response. "Doug?" she interjected in a deliberately quiet voice.

He looked up. "What did you say? I missed that last."

"You've missed the last several years if you ask me." She shoved her chair back, scraping it across the floor, and stalked out of the room.

He left on a business trip the next day. Laura never saw him alive again. They told her he died of a massive coronary in the back of a taxi in Dallas, Texas.

The minister's voice rose, "A time to rend, and a time to sew; a time to keep silence, and a time to speak . . ."

Laura glanced over at her mother again. Robey wouldn't look at her now. So much silence.

The crowd began to shuffle by. People patted her shoulder, shook her hand, half-whispering their sympathies as if they had to be careful not to wake the dead. When they were all gone, Laura stepped forward to the casket. She stared down at it, focusing on a single water drop, her mind empty now, her vision blurred to all but the silver-white sparkle there.

"Everyone's going to be looking for you, dear. Not polite to keep them waiting."

Laura turned to face her mother then. She stared into Robey's eyes, transfixed for a moment by the familiar hollow void. Nothing. As always, she stared into those cool reflecting pools seeing nothing but herself.

Laura turned back toward the casket one last time. She laid her ungloved, left hand on top. The gold and diamond rings sparkled like the droplets of mist on the coffin. She stifled a sigh as she dragged her hand across its surface, drawing a cascade of water droplets into a streaming puddle. Her hope, her will, her strength spilled away with it.

"Yes, Mother. I'm coming," she replied wearily.

God knows we wouldn't want to inconvenience others with our grief. A time to mourn, and a time for a nice meal. A time to die, and a time for people to comfort the widow with platitudes. A time for all the meaningless bullshit and drivel.

Laura shook her head, "Let's go, Mother, it's a time to perform, isn't it?"

She felt a surge of guilt rise at the tone of her voice, but she couldn't help herself. The emotion ebbed as remorse set in. Laura took Robey's arm then, gentler than she'd sounded and guided her toward the cemetery walkway.

But a spurt of self-righteous anger caused her to lift her head as she felt her mother's gaze again. The brief peripheral glance gave her a small sense of satisfaction at the unsettled look on Roberta Maitlin's face.

Chapter 2

Glen Porter

Sunday, July 10, 1960

"Curry, get your butt outta bed," Glen Porter demanded as he entered his brother's room and swatted him with a pillow. "We gotta get on the road. It's a long way to Lowgap. 'Les we find us a ride."

Glen was itching to get started. Once he'd found work he was ready to hit the road. Especially when he was feeling penned in. Sharing his room with a wife he hadn't planned on cooped him up like a Banty rooster in a hen house.

One morning, Glen had rolled over in bed to stare down the business end of a double-barreled shotgun. When all was said and done, he found himself married to Callie Parker. He was helpless to prove he hadn't been with her *that* way.

Now she was here living at his Momma's, and her stuff was everywhere. It was time to get away for a while. He needed to find more work anyway. He had a wife and *two* young'uns on the way, if Callie Parker was to be believed.

God strike me dead. If she really is pregnant, it ain't mine.

But Roberta Foster's baby, that one definitely was. He and Robey had been romantic ever since she'd turned seventeen. If he loved any girl enough to marry, it was Robey. But he hadn't been ready to settle down yet.

Now he felt stuck. Roped and tied. Damn frustrated.

"Why the hell we gotta get up so early?" Curry grumbled as he planted his bare feet on the plank floor.

"It'll take us long enough to get there as it is, but Momma wants us to take Loy," Glen scowled as he answered.

"Aww, damn it, why we gotta take the retard again? He don't do nothin' with his money but buy paper and pencils and stuff."

Glen knew how Curry felt. He didn't like to admit it 'cause Loy was kin, but it sure was inconvenient lookin' out for him all the time. Especially when they were out to have fun, which they surely would be on their way back home.

But their momma, Beulah Porter, insisted, "You boys gotta stick together. You remember that. Folks gotta take care of their own. It's blood that matters most."

Beulah raised them by herself after their daddy was killed in an accident at the mill. Glen was five at the time, Curry, a three-year-old terror, and Loy was born after her husband passed.

Time came, when they were old enough, Beulah insisted her boys get out and work for a living like men. With Glen as their leader, they took what jobs they could find and stayed at them for as long as they lasted. In the process, Glen and Curry worked up a powerful thirst for Johnny Bean's home-brewed white lightning, and a hankering for a pretty girl. And Loy? Well, who knew what Loy wanted?

Glen wondered now and then what went on in his little brother's head. There were times he looked like he was deep in thought, but that wasn't likely. There was a certain look he'd get when people were hurtful or mean, like he was sad and puzzled all at once. It was the same way he looked at Curry most of the time. But when he scribbled, his face changed. When he had pen and paper in his hands, it was hard to get him away from it. One more reason Curry got annoyed with him.

Well, no matter, if Momma wanted him to take his little brother along, he'd take him, and watch out for him the best he could.

CHAPTER 3

LAURA

Saturday, October 2, 2010

Laura wasn't sure how long she sat in the car, gaze fixed on all the stuff in the garage that they never used anymore. Ten-speeds chained to rusty racks, hunting rifles locked and lined up like soldiers at attention, horseshoes and posts piled in a dilapidated box along with a pair of corroded dumbbells. They used to do a lot of things together.

She missed the cool foggy mornings when they headed out into the local game lands to hunt. It might seem strange, but she liked the feel of a rifle in her hands, the weight balanced between them as she pressed the butt to her shoulder, the sulphury metallic taste in the air when she fired a round, the oily smell of a clean barrel.

A sudden shiver brought her back to the present. It promised to be a cold October.

Two months. Was it really two months since Doug died? She still struggled to focus. Everything was taken care of—phone calls, death certificates, lawyer visits. She'd have to keep working, but there was a little money set aside for retirement, and the house mortgage was paid. Yet somehow, nothing about life seemed settled.

With a sigh, Laura grabbed her groceries and headed for the dark empty house. She fumbled with the key in the lock. Bags and purse slid to the floor as she juggled an errant cell phone in midair to save it. She barely got in the door before the house phone rang.

"Hello?" she answered, her voice edgy. Laura raked her honey-brown hair back out of her face and studied her reflection in a window pane as she spoke. *God, she looked haggard.*

"Hello?" she tried again. No answer. But the line wasn't dead. Someone was there, she could hear him breathing.

"Hello, may I ask who I'm speaking to?" She softened her tone. This could be a client from Hannah's Hope. It was a day-services facility for mentally and physically disabled adults. Laura had worked there since her youngest daughter, Tara, was six. She was twenty-two now. Fresh out of college and off to start her own life as a teacher in Ohio.

A gravelly male voice stammered, "Laurie? I mean, is this Laura Allen Evans? I'm . . ." The caller broke into a harsh cough and the line went dead.

"What the . . .?" she declared, hazel eyes glinting as she glared at the handset.

Laura brought the phone to her ear once more, but he was gone. She dropped it into the cradle, her gaze still fixed on it. Something about the voice got her hackles up.

She glanced over her shoulder, a knee-jerk reaction, but Laura succumbed to the urge to check the house. She ended in the kitchen where she pulled the curtains shut. Both doors were locked and all was quiet, yet she couldn't shake the sudden, inexplicable weight of dread that came over her.

"This is stupid." Laura shook her head and sighed.

She grappled with the groceries, put out the trash, and changed into comfy leggings and a flannel shirt. Then, armed with a plate of leftovers and a glass of Moscato, she headed for the downstairs family room.

Laura ran an index finger across the movie titles in the DVD rack. Anything to get her mind off the emptiness. *Hope Floats? Does it really?* She grimaced as she popped the disc in the machine and glanced at the phone before sitting down.

The sweet white wine tingled in her mouth. She looked around the family room and her gaze stopped at the family picture gallery on the wall.

The brick rancher they'd bought the year after they married had four bedrooms, more than they needed for two children. Laura wanted to fill it with childish laughter, and she tried. They wouldn't even have had Barbara or Tara if she hadn't secretly skipped a few pills.

But now that she was alone she thought about selling. She always pictured herself in a rustic log cabin with gingham curtains on the windows, and tin spatter-ware on the table.

The house was another one of those decisions she'd let Doug make rather than argue. Laura found it less complicated to give in, or to simply do her own thing without approval. *Easier to get forgiveness than permission.* She realized too late the habit had eroded the foundation of her marriage.

She felt deceitful and wanted to be stronger than that. She wished she had been bold enough to choose her own way without apology. And loving enough to be straightforward with others— including her mother. But there was still time to change that if she could only summon the energy to care.

Laura sighed. She'd become numb and she wanted to feel. She wanted to cry, but she felt empty. Empty and alone.

She glared at the phone on the end table as it rang. "Hello," her answer was sharp and curt. "Who is this?" she demanded.

"Please, don' be mad. I been tryin' to . . ." the caller cleared his throat, then went on, ". . . tryin' to get up the courage to call you for a long time. There's so much I . . ." a coughing fit interrupted him again. "I need to see you. There's things I gotta tell you. I'm still here where I always been," he took a deep breath. "I love you, Laurie girl, and I'm real sorry 'bout . . . things."

Realization squeezed her with an icy grip. She recognized his voice, though the man sounded much older. But it couldn't be. He'd been missing for years. Somebody was messing with her.

Laura drew herself up to her full five foot two inches as she postured for a fight.

"Look, I don't know who you are or how you got this number, but this isn't funny. Don't call me again, or . . ." her voice caught as she grasped for a threat strong enough to scare off the boogeyman, but settled for a lame, "I'll call the police," and slammed the receiver down.

Laura wrapped her arms around herself tight. Her insides quaked and she trembled as the goosebumps rose on her skin. Her mother would say someone had walked on her future grave.

Robey had a southern, old-wives' tale for every occasion though she'd rejected that part of their lives long ago. She liked to tell people they were from Greensboro—the biggest city close enough to the unincorporated village of Grassy Creek, North Carolina, to be an acceptable white lie. It was the biggest city Laura's mother had ever been to before she lit out with her seven-year-old daughter for Pennsylvania.

But that voice, it had to be him. The one person her mother never wanted to hear anything about again. The one person Laura had longed to see just one more time. Her eyes welled up with tears as she shook her head in disbelief.

Seconds later the phone rang again. Laura paused and let out a deep sigh before she put the receiver to her ear. "Daddy?" she ventured. Her voice was small and distant to her own ears. "Daddy, is that you?"

"Oh, my little Laurie Allen," he answered. "I'm real sorry 'bout . . . things. I want to explain, but I cain't leave here," then he stopped to cough again. He drew a ragged breath and went on, "There's so much I need to tell you. Like as not they won't let me . . . but I gotta try . . ." There was a sudden electronic squeal like two microphones crossing each other, followed by loud static for a few seconds, and the line went dead.

Laura stared at the handset. What did he mean? *This is crazy.*

Frantically she dialed her mother's number, but stopped suddenly. It was late. Robey wouldn't be up this time of night. It would have to wait till morning. Tears stung her eyes but she held them in as she trembled.

"You're a grown woman, pull it together." Laura shook her head and sighed deep. She needed to settle down before she went to Robey with this. She couldn't let her mother think she was losing her grip on reality.

She kept looking at the phone, willing it to ring again. The movie was a done deal. She gave up and headed to bed to try to read. Eventually the book slid from her grasp.

Then there was something in the darkness, an ominous shadow she couldn't quite see. A little girl with blonde hair was lying on the cold ground, crying. Something dark and wet ran down the side of the child's face. Laura put her hand out to touch her. The shadow growled like an animal. Laura woke to the echo of a feral sound somewhere in the distance. The now familiar sense of dread weighed heavy on her limbs. It would be hard to settle back down.

But she finally drifted off again, thinking how strange it was that a person could live whole lifetimes in minutes while they slept, and how sometimes they weren't your own.

CHAPTER 4

CURRY PORTER

Saturday, August 20, 1960

The middle Porter brother stared at his reflection in a grey-tarnished mirror, razor blade poised.

The shack he and his brothers, Glen and Loy, shared with a group of nineteen other tobacco workers had one bathroom, one sink and a medicine cabinet. There was no toilet, though there were several outhouses for other necessities. But the harvest would be finished in a few days.

Curry Porter didn't mind the hard work, but he much preferred the recreation they'd find on the way home. He looked forward to that first swig of moonshine out of a brand new bottle.

"Bafroom," Loy interrupted Curry's contemplations.

"Yeah, yeah, gimme a minute, Loy boy," he grumbled at his brother and shut the door in his face.

Damn kid wasn't good for much. Took him longer than a sucker worm to make his way through a row of tobacco. 'Course he was fun to mess around with. Especially when it came to his little girlfriend. As retarded as he was, the two were quite a pair. Still, she was kind of sweet and innocent with her smooth, fair face.

Curry pulled the razor blade down the side of his cheek as his reflection wavered in the mirror. Then his eyes clouded over, his face twisted into a sneer and his yellowed eye-teeth glittered. For a second he didn't recognize himself.

But then his hand slipped and the razor cut into his jaw. "Goddammit!"

Curry grabbed a towel and wiped the blood. Then he stared, fascinated by the deep red flow as it spread to stain the pure white towel.

CHAPTER 5

LAURA

Sunday, October 3, 2010

The subject was taboo.

And Laura hadn't talked to her mother since the funeral. She took a sip of coffee. It was time to ignore the jangled nerves and pick up the phone. Odd thing was, most people considered Robey pleasant, polite, friendly. A woman who rarely let her feathers get ruffled.

Laura saw things differently. She knew her mother as cool, distant and unemotional.

Except for the few times Laura dared to ask about her real father. Then Robey's face would go pale like she'd seen a ghost. She'd yell at Laura to mind her own business, run off and shut herself away in her room for hours. When she would come out later, it was like nothing ever happened.

On the day they left North Carolina, Robey drove up to Aunt Hattie's in a beat-up, army-green station wagon and launched into a frightful tirade. She'd jumped out, slammed the car door, and marched right up to Laura's room. She threw a suitcase on the bed and went through the dresser, the closet, the shelves, stuffing everything into that ugly brown bag.

Her eyes were red and swollen and her dime-store mascara left black streaks on her face. "Stupid. So stupid. Never shoulda believed anything that man said. Just another stupid hick," Robey ranted as she threw clothing across the room. "We gotta get out of this godforsaken, backwoods, hillbilly hell before it's too late."

The words burned in Laura's memory. Her mother sounded so angry. She was shaky, her face pale and pinched. Laura still wasn't sure if it was rage or fear that had gripped Robey that day. But from then on, it was understood, they would never talk about anything that came before the move to Pennsylvania.

"Hello?" With a single word, her mother could manage to sound questioning and accusatory at the same time.

"Hello Mom, it's Laura. How are you?" Her own voice came out passive-submissive in spite of herself.

"Oh, I'm fine, thank you. And you?" Robey would be polite to a fault to keep a conversation light, and short.

"I've been better." *Understatement of the century.*

"Oh, really? What's wrong? I could send money if you need it." Roberta Maitlin might be emotionally remote with her family, but she would never let one of her own down if they needed financial help.

"No, I . . ." Laura hesitated a moment, "I had a couple of strange phone calls last night." She paused again, "I thought you might be able to help me sort them out."

"Phone calls? Me? Why, what makes you think I can help?" Robey sounded suspicious already.

Laura's voice faltered, "Because I believe . . ." she paused again, "it was Daddy."

"Oh, for heaven's sake," Robey huffed, "that's crazy." She paused a few seconds and took a deep breath before she went on. "He died years ago. Now you just put any thought of all that out of your head. It's ridiculous. Really," she emphasized the last word.

"No, Mother, you told me once they'd never found him. Was that true or not?"

"I—" Robey gave a heavy sigh. "Oh, why must you always come back to this? It's time to just let it go, Laura. Howard was your father," she delivered those last few words like a gavel pounding out final judgment on the matter.

Robey sighed again. "*I* think you're still upset over losing your husband," she declared with authority. "It happens. Life goes on.

This is no time to go digging up the past because of some misplaced emotional need."

"No. You didn't hear him." Laura took a breath and let it out before she went on. "Somebody's holding him against his will. He said, 'they' wouldn't let him talk to me." With that bit of news, Laura laid the foundation for her next announcement, "I'm going to North Carolina to look for him."

"No! You can't. I forbid it. I won't let you scandalize my good name dredging all that up again," Robey declared.

"I'm sorry you feel that way, but you can't order me not to go, Mom. I'm a grown woman. I've always hoped one day you'd tell me more about what happened. But if you refuse, then I'll just have to find out for myself." She waited for some response, but there was only silence. "I love you, Mom, but I have to know," Laura finished.

Robey hung up without saying goodbye.

CHAPTER 6

LOY PORTER

Thursday, September 1, 1960

Loy flinched and ducked as his brother reached for him.

Curry only draped a solid arm across Loy's shoulders and pulled him in close.

It was barely daylight. They were headed home from Lowgap. They'd worked six weeks on a tobacco farm to bring in the harvest. He was glad they were done.

Curry leaned in heavy on him and started talking, "You know what, Loy boy? I think it's time you learned somethin' about women." Curry made a twisty face when he said it. "See, I figure you already know how to handle the poker yourself. You just ain't ever learned nothin' 'bout how to use it to stoke a female's fire." Curry winked at him as he poked his first finger in and out of a circle he made with his other hand.

Loy pretended not to understand. He shrugged his brother's arm off and dropped back. He didn't like it when Curry talked about baby making that way. It gave him knots in his belly and a creepy, crawly feeling on his skin.

This was their third day on the road. It was a long walk. Glen told him they'd get home sometime tonight.

But he also said they had to stop at Johnny Bean's. They only went there to buy moonshine. He didn't like the way the moonshine made him feel. It gummed up his mind and addled his brain. He had enough trouble with his thoughts and words.

Sometimes Curry made him drink it, though.

Glen laughed when he did but mostly he put a stop to it pretty quick. Glen would never let things go too far.

'Course he knew his limits with them.

They were both mountainous tall. Over six foot each. And they were muscled, tough, hard men.

He was a pale little boy everyone called a retard.

His thick, short fingers made him slow and clumsy with his hands. And he was shorter by a head and shoulders than either of his brothers.

If they decided Loy had to do something, he had to do it. They'd proved it more than once.

All at once Curry stopped laughing. He got all serious. And his eyes got far away. "Ain't nothin' in the world like bein' with a girl. Every time I think about it, it makes my loins ache."

Loy knew what he meant. He had that swelling in his pants before.

He was beginning to feel it now. His face burned at the idea.

"Yessiree, Bob, you listen to me and you'll learn somethin' on this trip, little brother." Curry punched him hard in the shoulder then.

He might be slow, but instinct told him when to be wary.

His brother was working up an idea, and Loy didn't much like Curry's ideas.

CHAPTER 7

LAURA

Sunday, October 3, 2010

Family is complicated.

Roberta Maitlin hadn't simply walked away from the past, she'd cut her daughter off from the opportunity to know anything about her own. But Laura had done some snooping as an angst-ridden teen and come across an old Chicago roller skate box tied with string. There were odd pieces of ribbon, dried flowers, a movie ticket stub for *Ain't Misbehavin'*, a locket from Glen Porter, and a stack of black and white photos—the Robey in the box was not the woman Laura grew up with.

The most important thing she'd found was her birth certificate. The document read, *"Laura Allen Porter."* Even though they'd never married, Robey had given her Glen's middle and last name.

She sifted through the stuff and found a picture of her father and one of Aunt Hattie with her phone number on the back. She took them both. If her mother had noticed she never said so.

Laura went to the hall closet and pulled a shoe box of her own mementos down from the top shelf. Rifling through it she found what she was looking for.

"Hello?" Though the answering voice crackled with age, Laura was sure it was Hattie Perkins. She flipped the picture over to study the image. Her aunt had to be in her late 80s now.

"Aunt Hattie, this is your great niece, Laura. Robey's daughter. Do you remember me?" The years of disconnect suddenly hit Laura as she spoke.

"Laura? Laura Allen Porter? Is that really you?" Thankfully, Hattie Perkins' mind hadn't suffered with age. "Oh my lands, it's good to hear your voice. How are you? And how's your momma?" The woman sounded so pleased to hear from her, Laura was embarrassed at how long she'd neglected her.

"I'm—we're—okay I guess. We're both widowed now." Laura paused, it was the first time she'd called herself that. "But we're doing all right, all things considered. How are you?"

"These old bones are a bit creaky but that's nothin'. I'm real sorry to hear 'bout your husbands. I tried to get in touch with your momma for a long time. Never did hear from Robey." Hattie's voice faltered slightly.

"I know. I'm so sorry," Laura apologized.

"Aww, it's not your fault. I know Robey don't want to hear nothin' from any of us down here. I'm sure glad to hear your voice though. There somethin' special you called about?"

Laura hesitated before she spoke. "There is something I'd like to talk to you about." She paused and let out a breath before continuing, "It has to do with my father, Glen Porter . . . but I'd like to visit with you if I could?" she ventured.

"Oh my. Glen Porter, huh? Don't know if I'll be much good to you there." Hattie paused. "But there's others still here was close to him. Your uncles, Loy and Curry are still livin'. Loy ain't right though, and he don't talk much. And Curry, he's a hard one to nail down sometimes." The old woman went silent for a moment.

"Their momma, your granny Beulah's still livin', but she's up in age like me, and she can be a bit touchy. I cain't say for sure how she'd take to talkin' 'bout Glen." Hattie sounded dubious. "But I'd love to have you visit for any reason," the elderly woman concluded. She went on in a lighter tone, "And you're gonna stay right here with me too. You remember now, it ain't a fancy place, but I got plenty a room."

"Well, thank you, Aunt Hattie." Laura hated to be pushy but she felt an urgency to get moving. "Would Saturday be too soon?"

"You come on down anytime you want," Hattie Perkins declared.

Laura still held the shoe box on her lap as she hung up the phone. She spotted the photo of her father forever captured as she remembered him best. Glen Porter leaned against the front fender of a 1950's Ford that in its day must have been considered something else. It wasn't his. He'd never owned a car.

He was dressed in a plain white t-shirt with the short sleeves rolled up at the cuffs and a pair of washed-out blue jeans. He had a lean handsome face with a high forehead, and a dark wave of hair. He had a smile that transformed his face even in faded black and white. He wore black leather oxfords with a narrow toe and slight heel. Probably the only pair of new shoes he'd ever had, always polished to a shine.

Laura swore she could smell his cologne and feel his strong warmth as she sat on his lap. She recalled how he would wrap his strong arms around her and smooth her hair with one big, work-roughened hand. Laura couldn't believe how much she still yearned at times for the comfort and safety she'd felt in his arms.

"Oh, Daddy," she whispered.

Had he suspected something was going to happen to him? Had he known Robey planned to take off? Laura sighed deep. Nostalgia is heavy when it's wrapped in unsettled grief.

She knew it wouldn't be easy to get permission to take off work, but she was going with or without it. She called her manager, Shelly Davis. "I'll be gone at least a week, possibly more. Maybe I should take a leave of absence since I don't know how long I'll be," Laura ventured.

Shelley was unsympathetic. "Vacations are supposed to be submitted at least two weeks in advance. And we don't grant leave of absences. We're shorthanded," she declared. "You know we're hiring again. You might want to keep that in mind."

Leave of absences? Laura had to bite her tongue to keep from correcting her boss. She hated being confrontational. "I have to go," she finished simply.

"Okay. Fine," Shelley snapped. "One week. Any more than that . . ." the woman let the thought dangle.

Decisions made and details organized, Laura fell asleep almost as soon as she laid her head on the pillow. But deep in the night she came upon a lone little girl in a dark wood. The child clutched a baby doll. She could hear heavy footsteps and there was a strong odor of animal musk. The girl turned and beckoned to her with one short, pale arm. When she turned away Laura followed. The little girl kept looking back. The child's wide frightened eyes were focused on something behind them. When Laura turned to see what it was, she stumbled and a pressing weight came down on top of her.

She struggled to breathe. Her chest felt heavy, her body crushed. She woke with a start. Laura tried to shake off the feeling, but realized the little girl was the same one she'd dreamed about the night before.

CHAPTER 8

CARL EDWARDS

Monday, August 1, 1960

"You gotta see it's for the best, Carl."

Mamie Edwards pushed a pamphlet across the kitchen table toward her husband as he ate his breakfast of biscuits and gravy with a generous helping of grits on the side. He took a sip of thick black coffee and eyed the brochure. He knew what it was. They'd argued over the idea for days.

Carl Edwards also knew when his wife got something in her head she'd dog it like a hound on a blood trail. Especially when that something had to do with their only child, Lottie Mae.

He often feared Mamie didn't have the normal motherly instincts toward her offspring most women did. 'Course that was partly because the child had been born . . . different.

He'd known right away something was wrong. Mamie had the baby at home. The Doc got there in plenty of time and everything went fine, but the problem wasn't in the birth process. Doc had said it was because Mamie was older than most women when they had their firstborn.

She was thirty then and the baby had been a surprise. Mamie never wanted children, but she seemed to adjust to the idea once it happened. Carl, on the other hand, was twelve years younger than her and he'd looked forward to a family of his own.

"Da-da," Lottie called out, her eyes sparkling and her smile shining like the sun. "Sar-ha." She held up her new dolly with the blue dress. She hadn't let go of it once in the week since he brought it home for her.

"Yeah, honey. Sarah's a nice name." A soft smile curled his lips as he watched his little girl play.

He remembered cradling Lottie in his arms when she was still all new and wet. He'd loved her instantly in spite of her odd features. She was his beautiful, blue-eyed baby girl.

He'd realized early on how helpless she was. He knew she'd never marry or have a family to take care of. He knew she could never take care of herself on her own. But this idea of Mamie's, it seemed so cruel, so inhuman. He picked up the pamphlet finally and flipped through it. It wasn't like they could talk it over with Lottie to see how she felt about it. And he had the niggling feeling if she could understand it, she wouldn't want to have it done.

Mamie had gone to the doctor that delivered Lottie and asked what to do about the child's woman changes. He'd given her the information for a special doctor at the hospital in Raleigh who he thought could help. So she went off on the bus one day and came back hours later with a pamphlet and a plan. And she'd been determined to convince him it was for the best ever since.

His little girl was so innocent and it was for sure they couldn't be there to protect her forever. Maybe it was for the best in the end. If Lottie ever did get curious enough about how babies were made, it was possible there'd be another helpless innocent who'd need cared for all its life.

"It's hard enough takin' care of her like she is. How'd we ever take care of a young'un' of hers if it came to that too, Carl?" Mamie jarred him from his contemplations, echoing his own thoughts.

Carl Edwards gave a heavy sigh. "I don't know Mame, don't seem right." He looked down at his feet. "I see what you're tryin' to say. It's just . . ." and he sighed again, ". . . I hate to do somethin' to her she just wouldn't understand."

"She don't understand much of nothin', Carl. You know that. We been raisin' her near fourteen years. We both know she don't see the world like we do," Mamie argued. She pressed on, "And it would be in a hospital where they'd put her to sleep and she won't feel a thing. It'll be done, and she'll come home the next day. She won't remember nothin'."

Carl studied Mamie's face. The woman had that look she got when she was determined he should see things her way.

She filled his coffee cup again as she continued, "You know I had the same op'ration after she was born. Ain't no worse than your monthlies, and she's already gettin' those. And she still will, so she won't be no more, nor less the wiser to it all."

Carl Edwards hung his head and sighed. Finally, he looked up and gave his wife the answer she begged so hard for, "Alright, Mame, if you think it's for the best. And you're sure they won't leave her scared and hurtin'?" He looked his wife in the eye. "Go ahead then. Call that doctor in Raleigh. I'll take her down."

Mamie wasted no time. She got on the phone right away, and within a week Carl had taken their daughter to have the operation that would keep her from ever getting pregnant.

And though he couldn't have known it at the time, he'd torture himself over it for the rest of his days.

CHAPTER 9

LAURA

Saturday, October 9, 2010

Laura turned down the rutted dirt lane with a raised grassy hump running down its middle. She was glad now she'd allowed herself to give in to a sudden youthful urge to rent the red Jeep Wrangler 4x4.

A long, narrow field of large round bales of hay, bordered by a heavy copse of trees, ran along the right side of the road. There was a faded-out tobacco shed sitting at one end. She had a mental picture of the dark interior, bundles of yellow-brown leaves hanging from sticks laid across beams. For a moment she smelled the musty sweet scent of drying tobacco.

It hit her hard how long ago and far away it all seemed. Like it happened in another lifetime to someone else. She was from here; these were her roots. Yet, whether by choice or omission, she had so little memory of it.

Laura was only seven years old when they left, and it had been in such a hurry. She was sure she remembered a cloud of dust behind them as she'd looked back to wave at Aunt Hattie. She had no way of knowing it would be over forty years before she would see her again.

Laura suddenly felt like she was being watched. Something about the woods beyond the place beckoned to her. Something there danced on the edge of her memory, leaving her unsettled. And now, she felt as if it was closer than ever. As if that something was still out there—and it was about to catch up to her.

She pulled up to the little farmhouse at the end of the lane. Laura immediately recognized the plain wood-sided, two-story with peeling white paint and no railing on its front porch. She used to love to run off the high end, arms spread like a bird.

A tiny woman with a weathered, well-tanned face surrounded by a halo of soft, white hair stepped out to greet her. Laura caught her breath. Her heart went heavy with the weight of so many years gone by. The elderly woman descended the porch toward her, arms outstretched, and the years melted away.

In an instant she was the little girl who sat in her aunt's lap in the living room rocking chair as the older woman hummed and sang old folk tunes, or sometimes gospel music, in her ear. She had always smelled of lavender and rosewater, and she still did.

"Aunt Hattie, it's so good to see you again," Laura said as she stepped back and looked into those soft grey eyes.

People say you can't go home again, but somehow she felt as if she'd been destined to come back here, so much she needed to remember.

After Laura settled into the room she'd used as a child, Aunt Hattie invited her to "sit a spell," as she put it. She wanted to catch up over a cup of coffee and homemade chocolate chip cookies.

There were several picture albums in a stack on the table. One was open a few pages in. Laura studied the photos there, all black and whites. She recognized her mother, Aunt Hattie, a few others. There was one of Laura herself out by the tobacco shed holding a kitten behind its front elbows, its lower half dangling free.

There was another of a young couple that looked familiar. They stood in front of an old single-story cabin. It sat off the ground on stone footers so one end was higher up than the other, creating a sort of crawl space under the house. Its front porch was suspended above the ground and ran the whole way across.

Laura reached out to touch the picture, mesmerized as her mind drifted back in time. She'd been out and about exploring on her own, "chasing rabbits," her mother used to call it. That's when the man called to her to come help him.

A mountain of a man, big as a bear and hairy as one too. He had chickens that liked to go up under the porch to lay their eggs. His wife was too big with a baby inside her to get under the house for them anymore. And he was too big too, anytime.

"Hey there, young'un. Think you could get up under that end a the porch there and get them eggs for me?" The hairy man looked her in the eye when he spoke.

"I reckon I prob'ly can," she'd told him. She was tall for her age, but she was a slight little thing as Aunt Hattie always said.

"You that Porter girl, ain'tcha? Robey's young'un?" the man asked.

"Yessir," she answered and nodded her head, tangled curly tresses bouncing wildly. "I'll get them eggs," she told him.

She was sliding under the porch on her belly, an egg basket in one hand, when she'd seen it. A skull, with holes for eyes. And it had teeth.

Laura breathed in, shaking off the fear she felt again. Shocked by the sudden recall of details that had escaped her until now. . .

Aunt Hattie watched as she stared at the photo. Now she stepped up to look over Laura's shoulder. "That's Calvin and Edith Dillon. She was close to deliverin' their first baby in that picture. That was taken just after you . . ." the elderly woman trailed off.

But Laura nodded, "Go on, it's okay. I'd like to hear what you remember."

"Well, when you found those bones under the porch, they ended up callin' Sheriff Wilson."

Hattie shook her head as if she couldn't believe such a thing could happen.

Then the elderly woman went on, "His deputy was a skinny fella, cain't remember his name. But he crawled up in there and found the whole skeleton of a child. There was a doll in there with her, too. It's what made them suspect it was Carl and Mamie Edwards' girl, Lottie Mae. Let's see, she'd been missin' 'bout seven years by then. You were real shook up. But your daddy came by that evenin' as I recall and calmed you right down." Aunt Hattie interrupted herself to offer Laura more coffee and cookies as she stood and stretched her back.

Laura hoped they weren't finished, but she didn't want to wear the elderly woman out her first day here. She got up to help fill the cups and add cookies to the plate.

"I remember being scared and my father holding me in his lap that day," Laura prompted.

Hattie went on, "Strange too, 'cause he usually visited with you out on the porch, or took you for a walk or somethin'." She shook her head and frowned, "But that night he tucked you into bed himself. Then your momma followed him onto the porch. They were out there for a while. When she finally came in, she was awful upset. Never did say why.

"They investigated but eventually they claimed there just wasn't enough evidence to charge anybody for anythin'. 'Course in the meantime your daddy disappeared, and soon after your momma . . . well you know the rest," she finished.

Laura was so wrapped up in the story she felt let down when it was over. Was that all she would ever get?

"Aunt Hattie, when do you think I could meet Loy and Curry? And my grandmother, Beulah? And the sheriff? And what about Lottie Edwards' family, are there any of them around still?"

"Well, now let me see. Horton Wilson died years ago. His son Blaine is sheriff now though. He'd probably tell you what he can. He's a bit older than you, so he might remember more himself," the elderly woman offered. "I'll take you to see your granny, Beulah, and those boys if they're around. We'll go tomorrow after church service if that's all right with you. Beuly don't get around real well. She's near blind too, just so's you know."

The older woman studied the pictures in front of them for several seconds.

"As far as the Edwardses?" Hattie Perkins continued, "Hmm, I don't know, but I think maybe Carl's still livin'. Cain't be sure. 'Course the sheriff would probably know that, too. You can ask him yourself. His office is over in Jefferson. Ain't hard to find."

Laura bit her lip. "You wouldn't still have a phone book around would you?" she asked. "I could look it up myself." Her aunt opened a kitchen drawer and pulled out a thick, well-worn, yellow phone directory.

The two women sat shoulder to shoulder at the kitchen table as they browsed through the photo albums. They talked most of the afternoon and all through dinner. Together, they cleaned up and locked the house. They even climbed the stairs as one.

Laura tried to call her mother before turning in for the night. As the phone rang, she pictured Robey dancing her around this very bedroom holding both her hands. Her mother had been so happy back then. She was in love.

There was no answer.

Laura sighed and shook her head to dismiss the reverie then called her daughter Tara instead to let her know she'd arrived safely.

Between the trip down the highway, and the even longer trip down memory lane, her body was weary and her emotions drained. She was sure once her head hit the pillow she'd sleep like a rock.

And she did at first.

But somewhere in the night she found herself wandering through a dense forest. The moon was bright though the darkness weighed heavily. Then the little blonde girl took her hand. She held a baby doll tight in the other arm. Laura smelled the damp earth and rotting foliage. She felt the autumn chill on her skin.

Then she glanced back to see a huge wolf-like creature close behind them. It growled a deep, snarling growl. And it walked upright on thick hind legs as it loomed over her. Its hairy body bulged with muscle and sinew, its yellow teeth shone in the moonlight. The front legs were flexible like arms, and it had thick, hairy fingers where there should have been paws. And when it sprang for her she felt its hot breath, and smelled its feral stink before she woke, mouth open in a silent scream.

Laura hoped she hadn't cried aloud. She listened to see if she'd disturbed her elderly aunt. When she was sure all was well, she slid back down under the covers brooding. Was it possible the little girl in her dreams now was the one she'd found under the porch so many years ago? She hadn't seen a face, only brief glimpses of pale skin and shadowy eyes. She had no idea what the child had looked like in life. But Laura sensed something terrible had happened to the girl.

She wasn't convinced the spirits of the dead could communicate with the living. Still, she couldn't help but wonder if the girl in her dreams wanted to tell her something. It was a restless night. She fell asleep again at last, contemplating how horrible it must be to endure a violent death in silence.

CHAPTER 10

GLEN

Thursday, September 1, 1960

In spite of the cool night air, Glen's shirt was soaked with sweat. His palms were damp and his whole body shook. Things got out of hand after they left Johnny Bean's.

He was supposed to watch out for his little brother, but now Loy was off by himself in the woods, scared and hurt. Their momma would tan his hide for sure. It wasn't right what they'd done. None of it.

Glen had watched Curry's mouth twist into that familiar viscous snarl and the hair on his arms stood up. His skin felt like it was crawling with bugs. But it was too late to change any of it now. They had to get home and wait for Loy.

"C'mon," Glen ordered. His stomach lurched as he reached for the big rock on the ground beside them. "He'll head home soon as he's calmed hisself down. We gotta get movin'. We'll wait out at the shed and watch for him."

The two brothers took to the path home in the bright moonlight. But as they went, Glen stopped to throw the rock as far as he could out into the pond. The splash sounded loud in the quiet dark.

Glen was sure he'd seen a pair of yellow-amber lights in the trees on the other side before they winked out and disappeared.

CHAPTER 11

LAURA

Sunday, October 10, 2010

The Ashe County Baptist church stood at the bottom of the steep mountain slope that was its graveyard. Tombstones continued to spread upward, climbing toward heaven as its population had grown.

Inside the sanctuary, the handmade straight-backed wooden benches had been replaced with store-bought, padded pews but not much else had changed in the last forty years. The wooden attendance and offering board, with its plastic slide-in letters and digits, said the morning crowd had numbered 112 in all, and the offering came in at a modest $337.55.

The minister talked about how families should raise children to believe in something bigger and better than themselves. Good words, but the audience was comprised mostly of greying heads. Still there were a few young families. *Faithful hangers-on*, Laura thought, *struggling to find meaning in life.*

Aunt Hattie sat riveted on the preacher's words, head tilted to the side, a beatific look of peace on her face. She nodded her head continuously in agreement as he spoke. One of Laura's earliest childhood memories was sitting in the pew beside her aunt, watching her like she was now. She and her friends fidgeting to get outside and play.

There had been more children when she was young. And there had been more restless, childish noises in the sanctuary. At the sound of the last "Amen," they would burst out the back doors to run off and play among the trees in the cemetery.

Laura had a sudden urge to meander through the graveyard. But Hattie Perkins had other ideas as the service ended. She steered Laura through the center aisle and introduced her to everyone around them. Sister Hazel, Brother Galen, Brother Parker. Baptists used familiar family titles for anyone they considered one of them. At the back door she shook hands with the minister and exchanged friendly greetings. Aunt Hattie introduced him as the Reverend Cecil T. Honeywell.

She explained Laura was from out of town but she'd been born right there in Ashe County in 1960, which gave away her age, of course. But Hattie went further. She told him Laura was back to find out more about her daddy who'd disappeared when she was a little girl.

The reverend met and held her gaze for several seconds. Laura grew uncomfortable under his scrutiny. But he appeared genuinely interested in her story and asked if he could be of any help.

Laura didn't see how. He said they'd only moved to nearby Shatley Springs a few years ago. She thanked him and told him she'd keep it in mind. He reached to shake her hand a second time then, as he appeared to study her face once more. Laura smiled and nodded, anxious to move on.

Half an hour after services ended they finally made their way out the back door. Aunt Hattie needed to speak to someone else before they left, so Laura excused herself to take that walk through the cemetery.

The mountainside was bathed in the sharp clear-yellow of an early fall day as she climbed the cement steps and passed through a creaky wrought-iron gate. The spike-tipped iron fence went around three sides of the cemetery, while the back line near the top of the mountain was made of wire, as if to allow for expansion. All of it was rusty and pitted, and some sections leaned at odd angles.

She wandered through the stones as she read dates that went back to the 1700s, while some had worn so badly they were unreadable. Ascending the hill read like a historical record. Dates proceeded to increase like time marching up the mountainside.

Most of the markers bore short biographical epitaphs: *Died Unexpectedly of Influenza; Beloved Daughter, Wife, and Mother; Stillborn Son of Hannah Purcell; Best Smithy in Three Counties.*

At last she came to names she recognized. She located her grandfather's headstone and she found Lottie Edwards'. It had a lamb carved into a circle in the top center. The etching read, *"Lottie Mae Edwards, Beloved Daughter of Charles and Mamie Edwards, Born October 24, 1946—Died September 1, 1960."*

Eerie, she thought. Lottie had died the day Laura had been born.

What she truly hadn't expected to find was a stone bearing her father's name. The small, plain marker read, *Glen Porter, July 18, 1940—October 10, 1967.* It gave her a sudden chill. She wondered who'd put it there. Laura glanced down the hillside toward the gate and spotted Aunt Hattie waving for her. She waved back and headed down the slope, but stopped suddenly, jerking her head toward the woods. Someone, or something disappeared the moment she turned. She searched the tree line, waiting. Adrenaline shot stinging needles through her. She took a deep breath and deliberately set her eyes on the ground ahead as she hurried to join her aunt.

Laura had driven the rental Jeep to church. Her aunt had a car but rarely drove anymore, except for her every-other-week grocery trips to town. She usually got a ride to church from neighbors.

"Take a left down here at the stop sign onto Grassy Creek Road," Aunt Hattie directed. "Then it'll be about a mile or so to Old Highway 16. You'll turn right like you're goin' back to my place. Then just up the road a piece, you'll make another right on Porter's Hollow Road." Aunt Hattie appeared to enjoy her role as navigator.

Laura glanced over at the elderly woman and a nostalgic sense of regret overwhelmed her. She thought of all she had missed not growing up here with this gentle soul to help raise her. She also felt a sudden surge of irritation with her mother for preventing it.

Her mother's penchant for presenting what she felt was an acceptable social appearance annoyed Laura. But at that moment, it went so much deeper. She also had a grandmother here she'd been taken away from, and uncles too. She felt she'd been cheated out of a priceless heritage. And why? Because of Robey's own ambitions, her own bitterness.

But then, what had prevented her from getting in touch with her aunt, or the others, on her own over the succeeding years? Easier to blame her mother for her own lack of courage and determination.

Porter's Hollow Road was a mile-long rutted stone road that ran through a sharp cut between two mountains, barely wide enough for two cars to pass each other. A narrow stream ran along one side, and a small network of lanes cut off the main road. One disappeared out of sight in the trees as it climbed the mountain to their left and rounded a bend. Apparently Beulah's wasn't the only family that ever lived in Porter's Hollow.

The road suddenly ended in a wide turnaround, and just ahead, built into the base of a mountain that surrounded it in a sort of semicircle, was a modest clapboard built in two sections with opposing roof angles. The house was plain white except for the slate grey porch floor. The entrance straight above the steps was tucked into a corner, made where the two sections of the house met.

"Beuly's husband, Ervin, used to own the sawmill in town. She lives here with her youngest boy, Loy. He's physically capable enough, but his mind's another thing. The other one, your Uncle Curry, don't live here no more, but he can sometimes be found hangin' about," Aunt Hattie climbed the steps as she talked about the other woman, and made no effort to keep her voice down.

She knocked hard on the door frame with the side of her closed fist, saving her arthritic knuckles. Laura heard a slow rhythmic, *thump, thump, thump*, like someone tromping up steps.

Then a softer shuffling sound stopped in front of the door. It creaked open a few inches and a woman's weathered face appeared.

"Mornin' Beuly, it's Hattie Perkins here. How you doin' today? Thought I'd stop by after church and bring you a basket lunch," Aunt Hattie's voice went up a few volumes when she talked to the other elderly woman.

"Oh, well then, you come on in." Beulah Porter's voice was weak but clear. She was about four feet tall and bent over at the shoulders. Wispy grey hair escaped its loose bun giving her a disheveled look. But her midcalf-length dress was pressed and tidy, as was her pale blue, gingham apron. And she wore neatly fitted stockings with thick-soled, shiny black shoes.

"I brought you another visitor. This here's Laurie Allen. You know, my Robey's daughter. You remember Robey, now don't you?" Aunt Hattie reached for Beulah Porter's arm as she spoke. They turned toward the kitchen.

"What? Robey, you say?" she answered tilting her head and scrunching her nose. "Ain't heared nothin' a her in years. What you sayin'? She here with you?"

"No. Beuly, this here's her little girl. Laurie. You remember Glen's baby girl, don'tcha?" The volume of Aunt Hattie's voice increased with Beulah's expression.

"Oh, oh my lands, yes, yes. These old eyes a mine done got so dim I barely see the shadows of folks anymore. You say she's here with you? Now?" Beulah Porter turned her head in Laura's direction and reached out a bony arm.

"Yes, ma'am, I'm right here." Laura took the woman's hand. Beulah clamped onto her and drew her forward with more strength than Laura thought possible. The old woman's expression was hard as she tilted her head up. Laura was mesmerized. Those milky blind eyes were blank, but it felt like the woman was looking into her soul.

Aunt Hattie set the basket on the table and beckoned for Laura to help. The moment eased. Then they all settled around the table to eat.

There were sandwiches made of thick slices of baked ham on homemade bread, slathered with creamy pure white butter, and ham and bean soup with potatoes that they reheated on Beulah's stove. The smell from the steam rising off the pot made Laura's mouth water. And, as if that wasn't enough, Hattie Perkins topped it all off with a fresh apple pie she'd made earlier that morning.

The women chatted as they ate—about the weather, the church service, how the older ladies' bones ached more when there was a storm coming. Laura was anxious to get down to the reason they'd come. Then she caught sight of a flash of red plaid and blue jeans as someone passed through the other room. When she looked up she saw a shadow on the floor by the door frame. She could hear breathing, and someone gave a light cough to clear his throat. She wondered how long he'd been in there listening.

"Loy, that you, boy? Come on out here and meet Laurie Allen. This here's Glen's little girl come back to visit us. Come on now, don't hide. She come a long way to meet us," Beulah Porter commanded.

Loy peered around the door post. He had a pudgy, pale face and wispy grey-black hair swept across his balding pate. As he walked he tucked his shoulders forward and dropped his head like he wanted to fold his body in on itself. Everything about the man looked as if he was trying to disappear from the world.

"C'mon now, boy, come say hello to our visitors," Beulah's words pulled him forward as he inched along.

"How'y," his voice croaked and he mispronounced the word, leaving out the 'd'. But it was the only word his visitors would get.

Aunt Hattie got up to make him a plate of food, which he accepted with a nod. Then he waved a hand and shuffled out of the room without a backward glance. Laura watched as he sat down on the sofa in the next room in front of a long, low coffee table. From the blue glow that flashed across his features she could tell the TV was on.

The table was spread with papers, pencils, crayons. Loy sat his plate down carefully and picked up a marker with his left hand. He slid down to sit on his knees closer to the table, laying his elbow across the paper as he drew. The sandwich dangled from his right hand, bits of bread and ham falling on the page.

Laura had a sinking feeling. She wasn't likely to get Loy Porter to tell her much. She looked back at Aunt Hattie. The older woman must have interpreted her expression.

"Beuly, Laurie here and me, were wonderin' if you maybe had some recollection of what happened to Glen and your boys all them years ago? You know, when Glen up and disappeared."

Not too subtle a transition, but there it was. The question Laura wanted to get to all along. She watched Beulah's face as she let the thought sink in. The hard expression came back and the older woman's brow furrowed deep.

She started in slow, "Oh, my—that was s'long ago." She paused and Laura thought for a moment the elderly woman would refuse to tell them, or didn't remember.

Then she sank down into her chair further and tilted her head back. Closing her eyes, she spoke, "I 'member it like it was yesterday. Loy came wanderin' in the house early mornin' after bein' gone a couple a days. Could hardly speak a word. Tried, mind you. Hemmed and hawed and stumbled all over his-self."

Beulah paused, rocking her upper body gently as she appeared to collect her thoughts.

"Asked him where Glen and Cur was, but he just shook his head and cried. Sheriff showed up at the door later that mornin'. Tried talkin' to him too, but Loy didn't say no more. Sheriff told me he was lookin' for the other two to talk to 'em 'bout that little girl'd been found. By you, if I 'member right."

Beulah turned, tilted her head and appeared to look right at Laura. Her unseeing milky eyes glittered.

"I told him I feared somethin' bad happened to all of 'em," she finished.

Laura heard a shuffling sound and glimpsed Loy peeking around the door frame in the next room again.

Beulah went on as if she hadn't heard him. "He come back later that day, said he'd found where they'd been, but no sign a either of 'em. Found a lotta blood though, and some kind of strange tracks he couldn't figure out. Said if I seen or hear'd from 'em to let him know."

Laura watched Loy in her peripheral vision as his mother talked. He stayed close, his forehead bobbing around the door frame every few seconds.

"Cur finally showed up alone nigh on a week later. Come walkin' through the door pretty as you please. Said he didn't rightly know what happened. Couldn't 'member a thing." Beulah shook her head. "That's it. That's all I know, and all anybody ever did as I recollect." Beulah thumped her wrinkled fist on the table. "And there's done been enough rumors and hearsays about what folks think might a happened. But I say, let it be. Let my Glen rest in peace."

Laura drew back at the sudden vehemence. She had become so wrapped up in the story. Disappointed at its ending once again, she decided to brave her next question. "Miss Beulah—"

Her grandmother interrupted her, "You can call me Beuly, or Granny if you choose," she offered though her expression was anything but warm. It felt like permission out of a sense of obligation.

For the time being, Laura went on without using either, "Is there any chance I could talk to Curry myself?"

"Well, now, he's here somewheres. Out cuttin' wood, I think. He's got a place a his own over to Lansing, though. Comes by when he ain't too busy, helps take care a things. You could come back tomorrow mornin' if you got the notion," Beulah offered. "Should be stackin' the wood by then."

Laura thanked her, then she and Aunt Hattie cleaned up the meal, gathered everything together and headed out to the car.

When Laura opened the driver's door, she glanced up at the house and caught sight of Loy's pudgy face peering at her from the edge of a curtain upstairs. He caught her eye briefly, but then dropped his head and faded back into the room.

48

CHAPTER 12

CURRY

Thursday, September 1, 1960

Crouched beside a tree in the early purple twilight, Curry lifted his chin and tilted his head like a hound checking the air for sound or scent of its prey. A twig snapped. Then several in slow succession under heavy footfalls. Loy was finally back.

Curry gave one long and two short whistles to signal he'd caught wind of their brother. Glen slipped up beside him. When Loy passed close by, they rose and each took one of his arms and half-dragged him toward the shed. They both held a finger to their lips to silence him.

Inside, Glen sat Loy down on a stool and talked to him low and calm. Curry couldn't hear the words. He was posted at the door. But Loy sat quiet and listened as Glen worked. His face was dirt streaked, tears ran down his cheeks and he was white as a sheet. He stared up at Glen wide-eyed and his hands shook when he took the rag offered him.

Curry had a bad feeling about this. Loy was going to spill the beans and get them all in trouble if they didn't do something about it. And just whispering in his ear to be a good boy and keep it all a secret wasn't going to be enough.

"Boys! Glen, Curry, Loy, that you this hound's been barkin' at?" Beulah Porter let Rebel out the back door as she hollered for her sons. She couldn't see well anymore, especially not from that far away.

Curry saw it as his chance, "Glen, Momma's hollerin'. Why don't you go keep her busy? You're better at talkin' your way out of trouble with her than me."

Glen looked back and forth between his brothers. Loy sat staring straight ahead. He made no sign he'd heard anything. "Well, all right then. But get him cleaned up and don't do nothin' to excite him. He's got paper and pens over on the work table. Maybe they'll calm him down 'fore he has to see Momma."

"Sure Glen, I'll take care of him." Curry stood beside Loy and pulled a comb out of his own pocket. Glen left then.

Curry raked the comb through Loy's tousled mop of hair methodically. "You gonna calm right down now, ain't you, little brother? No need to go upsettin' Momma. Her heart ain't as strong as it used to be. She might feint dead if she knew 'bout last night. You wouldn't want to be the cause a Momma up and dyin' that way, would you?"

Loy's eyes got wider and he shook his head hard.

"Yeah, you cain't lose Momma. She means too much to you, don't she?"

Loy nodded vigorously.

"'Sides, you don't want to see me get mean neither, do you, Loy boy?" Curry sneered as he gripped Loy's shoulder and dug his fingernails into the younger boy's skin. Any more pressure and he would have drawn blood, but Momma would never see the bruises hidden under his shirt.

CHAPTER 13

LAURA

Sunday, October 10, 2010

Nostalgia is a powerful influence.

A Sunday drive around the area after church brought back memories. Eating homemade ice-cream, catching crawdads in the creek, skipping stones on a pond, things were coming back to her. And the heartache of loss grew.

When they got home Laura decided she needed to get out for a hike. Aunt Hattie wanted to take a nap. But that was fine. Laura preferred to explore on her own. The old cabin where she'd found the little girl's bones wasn't far from Hattie's.

She changed into jeans and a Pearl Jam t-shirt, grabbed a black and white flannel, tugged it on and rolled up the sleeves. Then she pulled on her favorite Timberland boots. They were a staple when she took to the woods, along with a hunting knife, a pair of gloves for clearing brush, and the hickory stick with the beaded leather horsehair braid at the top. Hiking was the one hobby she'd never given up, and always prepared for when she traveled.

The afternoon sun was high and warm. Birds twittered all around her and there was a slight northerly breeze. If it hadn't been for the shadow of her father's past that brought her back here, she might simply have enjoyed a good hike in the mountain air. But the weight of the years of secrecy bore down on her as she walked. In spite of the beauty of the day, the feeling increased as the woods grew thicker.

She heard a hawk cry. Searching the sky, she spotted it soaring above the tree tops. Laura caught her breath. *So beautiful, their cries so haunting.*

"Kee-aaaaa! Kee-aaaaa!" It cried again. She followed it with her eyes till it passed out of sight. Then her gaze trailed downward toward the path ahead where she spotted a gap in the trees. There was an opening to the left of the road where a lane had once been, now overgrown, but passable. Her pulse quickened as she turned onto the obscured trail.

The air got chillier. Laura pulled her flannel shirt closed, unrolled the sleeves and buttoned them. At last, the rugged lane made a bend to the right and ran into a tangle of brush. Inside all the bramble was a single-story log cabin left to be reclaimed by the woods.

She struggled through the undergrowth to get a better look. It was strangely darker here, the cabin swathed in shadow. She tested her weight on the bottom step, then thought better of it and backed down. Moving along the front she saw the sagging porch was still high enough off the ground to look under. But when she did, a sudden image of the little girl's skeleton flooded her mind and she jumped back.

Her heart was already racing when something crashed through the woods to her left. She could tell it was large, but she couldn't make out any details, just a dark, bulky shape. It moved fast, not even trying to be quiet.

Laura slowed her breathing and stood still, not wanting to give herself away. But the noise stopped as suddenly as it began. She held her breath and listened. Then, quiet as she could, she ducked low and crept around the side of the old house along the wall to the back corner.

She was about to rise up and peek around to get a better look when an eerie wail split the air beside her. The squalling, moaning, drawn-out, "why-y-y-y-y," sounded like a girl's voice.

Whatever was in the trees took off at a run now and disappeared, and the woods went silent. Even the birds stopped chirping. Laura's skin crawled, and her scalp tingled. She stood frozen in anticipation for several minutes. But there was nothing more. At last, the breeze returned and the birds began to sing once more.

She turned to leave, deciding not to explore any further for now. As she passed by the front of the house again, she saw a piece of paper tagged to a nail on one of the porch posts. It hadn't been there earlier. Laura glanced around before pulling it down. The words were printed immaturely in black marker.

"LEVE HEER! GO HOM! DON COM BAK!"

CHAPTER 14

CURRY

Monday, October 10, 1967

It's sure your sins will find you out, Momma always said.

Curry hiked a jug of moonshine over his shoulder and tilted it to his lips to drown out the thought. Then he passed it to Glen. He grabbed Loy by the sleeve and pulled him out of the shadows.

"You're comin' with us," Curry growled at him. "Your fault we's in this mess. You hadn't a hid that girl up under that porch, she'd a been dragged off by animals or somethin' back then."

Curry watched Glen take a long draught of the fiery liquid and swallow slow. His eyes watered something fierce. He opened his mouth but no sound came out.

A few seconds later, Glen snapped, his voice loud in the dark night. "Shut up, both a you. We gotta do some talkin', and some thinkin'. Let's get goin'."

They set off down the road with no particular direction in mind. But their feet found the path to the pond. And it was here Curry started to argue his view about who was at fault for what, and who was guiltiest.

Loy hung his head and stared at the ground. Glen kept shaking his head but he had little to say.

"They're gonna find somethin' to hang us with. I'm tellin' you, Glen. We coulda got outta this trouble if you hadn't a killed her. Wasn't necessary to go that far. Now somebody's gonna hang for sure. Somebody's gotta do the right thing here. I ain't no killer, but you, Glen . . ." Curry Porter accused, ". . . they's blood on your hands," he finished and glanced down at them as he spoke.

55

He didn't mean for real, but Glen lifted his hands in front of his face. His eyes widened, his mouth dropped open, and he rubbed his hands frantically on his shirt and pants. When that didn't satisfy him, he wiped them in the grass. Then he stumbled to the pond nearby to wash.

But in the middle of the argument, a low guttural growl came from the trees behind them and all three went dead silent. The hair on the back of Curry's neck began to prickle with anticipation. He knew what was coming.

Glen just stood there, hands dripping cold water in the eerie night. Neither him nor Loy so much as breathed aloud. But as they all listened, stiff and silent, the beast was moving closer. Curry could feel it in his soul. And the familiar stench of animal musk filled his nose and stung his eyes.

If the others didn't run, they'd die. He was sure of it. He couldn't let it hurt his brothers. Curry spun toward the trees and lifted the moonshine jug in the air as a weapon.

Loy found his feet then. He ran like he was being chased by the devil himself, screaming all the way. Glen stood and watched him disappear down the path by the pond.

Then there came a loud crashing through the trees, and a dark, hulking shadow blocked the path. It stood head and shoulders above them. Its eyes went from yellow-gold to burning-red in an instant. Its hot breath filled the air with steam.

The creature headed toward them. Glen stood frozen in place. Curry yelled at the last second for his brother to run. But the beast covered the distance between them in two steps. Huge claws extended, it attacked in an instant, ripping Glen's shirt clean off him with a single swipe.

Glen looked down at his chest, torn and bleeding, as the creature struck again. It tore at his face, his arms, his legs. He fell to his knees bleeding from everywhere. Then he collapsed forward into the dirt as it tore at his back.

Curry couldn't move. He gawked in morbid fascination as his brother's blood ran black in the moonlight. But as quick as the beast attacked, it stopped. Glen tried to move, but Curry got to him quick then. "Stay down. For God sakes, stay down," he snapped.

He glanced up then to look for the creature. It stood at a distance among the trees watching and waiting in the shadows. Glen gave up and laid his face in the dirt. At last his eyes closed and his body went still. The creature turned and disappeared into the woods.

Glen flopped onto his back as Curry rolled him over, but made no move to get up. He was out cold, bleeding all over, his clothes in tatters. Curry touched him gently on the one spot on his shoulder where he wasn't oozing as he tried again to stir him.

The jug of 'shine lay glittering in the moonlight where Curry dropped it. Unbroken, still half-full. He reached for it, sucking down a huge swig. Then he lifted Glen's head and put the bottle to his lips.

His brother sputtered and swallowed. He was alive at least.

Curry checked around once more to make sure the beast was gone for now. When he felt sure, he took Glen by the arm that was least damaged and pulled. "You gotta get up, Glen. We gotta get outta here," he whispered desperately. "Come on, I'll help you," and with that he put his own shoulder under Glen's arm and heaved.

Somehow Curry managed to get him on his feet, and started down the path away from Porter's Hollow. They couldn't go home like this. He'd find somewhere for his brother to hole up until they could figure out what to do.

That's how they ended up several miles further into the woods, back up at the old Hadley cabin. When the old woman who'd lived there died, the county had her buried in a pauper's grave and the place had been abandoned. The path into it was rough and overgrown.

The sky was starting to lighten by the time they stumbled through the door. Glen had fallen many times along the way, lost consciousness more than once. But Curry kept giving him swigs of the moonshine for the pain. Now he deposited his brother on an old wood-framed bed with a stinky feather-tick mattress on it. He set about pouring moonshine on the cuts while Glen screamed and passed out again.

His own head throbbed from the whiskey as he peeled away the scraps of clothing stuck to his brother's wounds and cleaned him up the best he could. Meanwhile he formed a plan.

There was an old rain barrel by the door with some water in it. He could clean himself up, go into Piney Springs and get some supplies: medicines, food, a change of clothes for Glen. It wouldn't take much.

So happened, that's where Glen's boy lived. The one nobody else knew much about. Tom would want to help his daddy. Glen always took care of him. He was young, but he was a strapping boy, big enough to carry feed sacks and hay bales all day. He and Tom could take turns doctoring Glen.

He'd worry about what was next when the time came.

CHAPTER 15

LAURA

Monday, October 11, 2010

Laura spent another sleepless night in half-waking dreams.

She saw the little girl in the blue dress wandering the woods in the moonlight. Then someone else was beside her, close. She knew it was a man, but she couldn't see his features.

The child looked back over her shoulder at Laura, big blue eyes full of fear. The man put his arm around her and drew her off the path. As he did, his form slowly swelled in stature, and the stink of animal musk permeated the air.

Laura saw the girl's features clearly this time. Panic filled her. She sensed if the child went with him she'd never come back. Then suddenly, Laura became the child and the man was pushing her to the cold, damp ground, his weight coming down on top of her. She couldn't breathe.

Laura woke gasping for air. She could still feel the creeping chill on her skin and the panic, feeling she was about to be—*what?*

Her hair was tousled, her nightshirt in a twist around her waist, the covers askew. Laura ran a hand through her rumpled hair and sighed. She needed coffee. Strong, hot, black coffee. Aunt Hattie was busy in the kitchen. The pot was already brewing and the smell of country sausage frying in the pan, and homemade biscuits baking in the oven made her stomach rumble. Southern hospitality wreaked havoc on the diet.

"Have yourself a cup a coffee and set up to the table. Breakfast's just about ready." Her aunt made it a cheery order.

Hattie Perkins was always wide awake first thing in the morning. *"Bright eyed and bushytailed,"* Robey would have said.

Laura glanced around the cozy house trying to remember her in this setting. How had she interacted with Aunt Hattie, Glen Porter? Robey had been so different then—friendlier, warmer, gentler. Laura had given up trying to find that woman again in her mother's eyes.

Every time she tried to prompt Robey to open up and talk about it, she would close up like a mimosa leaf. In the seven or eight hours it had taken them to go from North Carolina to Pennsylvania Robey had put on a mask that would not come off, and erected a wall that could not be scaled.

"You still plannin' on drivin' over to Beuly Porter's today?" Aunt Hattie cut into her thoughts.

Laura nodded, "I'll go on into Jefferson and do some other exploring then. I checked the phone directory. There was a Carl Edwards at a Jefferson address. I'd like to find out if there's some connection between Lottie's death, and my father's disappearance."

Laura realized she hadn't yet told Aunt Hattie about the note. She didn't want to burden the older woman but it might affect her too. She pulled the paper out of the pocket of her robe and asked her aunt to look at it. "Do you recognize the printing?" she asked.

"Cain't say I do." Aunt Hattie frowned, holding the paper at arm's length to read. "Don't make sense. Don't know who'd be *that* upset about you bein' here."

Laura hesitated. She didn't want to invent trouble where it didn't exist. But Glen Porter insinuated someone wouldn't let him see her. She pressed on.

"My father went missing, and now here I come all these years later saying I've heard from him and I want to find him. Maybe someone else had something to do with his disappearance, and that someone doesn't want me to figure it out. I know it sounds far-fetched, but it would begin to explain some things."

Aunt Hattie set a plate full of sausage and eggs, and fluffy buttermilk pancakes in front of her. She'd piled the biscuits into a stoneware bowl and set them on the table. There was homemade apple butter, Hattie's own strawberry preserves, and thick King Syrup on the table to top it all off. She could have fed a family of six on the meal the woman had cooked up for the two of them.

"Aunt Hattie," Laura breathed in, "you're going to send me home fat as a cow," she declared.

The older woman beamed. "You don't eat enough to keep a bird alive. You eat up, put some meat on those bones," she said. "'Sides, I'll make a plate or two up for you to take over to Beuly's. She can heat 'em up when she wants. Might warm her up to you some."

Hattie Perkins scrunched her face up like she was thinking hard. "You goin' into Jefferson, you probl'y oughta go by the sheriff's office and show that note to him." She fell so easily into a motherly role.

It warmed Laura's heart to be fussed over. "I hadn't thought about that. I guess I should. Thank you—for everything." She put her plate in the sink and turned to hug her aunt. "I should have come back to see you sooner, just to spend time with you."

"Oh, don't you worry about the past. It's enough to have you here now. I don't blame you or your momma for needin' to make a life for yourselves. You've done well—both of you." She squeezed Laura back. The two women worked together to clean up the dishes and the conversation flowed as easy as the water.

When Laura stepped out of the shower later she heard voices downstairs. She didn't mean to eavesdrop, but her curiosity was piqued. It sounded like the minister. Laura got dressed quickly. Picking up her digital camera, a black hoody and an extra flannel shirt, she opened the bedroom door as quietly as she could and paused.

"Cain't keep holdin' all these secrets." It was Aunt Hattie's voice. "You think she could get hurt? Really?" she heard her aunt ask.

The floorboards creaked under Laura's feet and the conversation took an obvious turn.

"Well now, Hattie Perkins, don't you be a stranger. I know you can drive that old car you got out there in the shed. You come for dinner and bring your niece with you. Elizabeth's hankering to talk to another female from somewhere other than Ashe County." The preacher turned a big brilliant smile on her as she walked in the room. "Good morning, Miss Laurie."

Laura bristled inside, but she shook his hand. His direct gaze unnerved her. It was like he expected something from her.

Laura smiled back politely. "Good morning, Reverend Honeywell. Nice to see you again so soon," she dropped the not-so-subtle hint that she suspected his motives.

"My wife insisted I stop by and invite you both to dinner. I was just telling your Aunt Hattie how Elizabeth felt terrible she missed you at church." The Reverend Honeywell looked her in the eye.

"I wouldn't want to impose," she replied.

"No such thing down here. If you're anybody's family, you're family to us all. 'Sides, I'm sure you've discovered we love to feed our visitors," the preacher quipped.

"Well, if Aunt Hattie is up for it, I'll be glad to drive," Laura glanced between them.

"Alright then, y'all come by tomorrow afternoon, say around four o'clock, and we'll visit a spell before supper." The Reverend Honeywell's grey-blue eyes sparkled when he talked. He smiled with his whole face, and he could mimic a southern drawl with ease. Laura wasn't sure it was entirely put on.

"That'll be just fine, Preacher," Aunt Hattie answered for them.

"Ladies," the minister pretended to tip a hat he didn't wear, and nodded to them both.

Then he ducked his head as he got into his truck, his black hair brushing the door frame. He looked their way and that smile took over his face again as he waved and turned the truck around.

Laura shrugged off her thoughts. "I guess I'd better get going. I'll call you later and let you know if I can't make it back in time for supper."

"You be careful now. I don't know, I'm just startin' to worry." Hattie Perkins shook her head and sighed, eyebrows drawn.

"I'll be fine," Laura assured. "I'll go see the sheriff right after I talk to Curry Porter." Laura went to her great aunt and hugged her, "I'll keep in touch, promise."

CHAPTER 16

CURRY

December, 1967

Glen sat in a straight-backed rocker near the cold fireplace hearth. He hadn't bothered to light so much as a candle as dusk closed in on the tiny two-room cabin. He rocked in a steady creaking rhythm. Bony hands clamped over the ends of the arm rests.

His fingers were turning blue and his breath came out in tiny, raspy wisps of steam. His gaze appeared to be fixed on the burnt logs in the hearth where black soot lined the walls and base.

A sudden fit of coughing racked his body so hard he raised both knees up to the chair arms. His feet hung in mid-air as they jerked out and back with each hacking bark. When they hit the floor again his body returned to the same fixed rhythm. A moment later, however, he jerked his head to the left and all motion ceased when Curry closed the cabin door with a scrape.

"Dammit, Glen. Why cain't you at least light the lantern? So damn dark in here I cain't see my hand in front a my face." Curry set the groceries on the floor and stumbled to the sink.

He flicked a cigarette lighter to locate the lantern underneath. When the flame flickered up, he let the globe down over it and set it on the single table in the room. Then he turned the wick higher and unloaded the groceries. It was never much, but it was enough to keep body and soul together.

"An' why ain't you got a fire goin'? We got all that wood cut and stacked right outside. They's plenty. No need to skimp on it," Curry complained. "Go on now, get up and get that fire a goin'."

Glen stared at him a moment longer then pushed his thin body up out of the rocker. Another fit came over him so hard it sounded like the croup. He bent over and put a fist to his mouth. When it was done, he lit a cigarette and shuffled toward the door. Curry shook his head and came to join him. He lit up too and they smoked in silence on the porch, then gathered a few logs each.

As they started the fire, Glen wheezed and whooped some more. Curry stopped to study him. This time the hacking bent him over to the floor on all fours and he coughed up bloody phlegm.

"We gotta stop movin' you all around. Them caves is too cold and damp for a man with your ailments. 'Course these drafty old cabins ain't much better."

Glen stared at his brother, mouth puckered and eyebrows drawn. Suspicion was etched all over his face.

"I'm the one keepin' you out of jail, big brother. It's a good thing Loy cain't talk an' I'm the only other one knows what you done. You 'member that, you hear?" A snarl played at the corner of Curry's mouth before he slammed the cabin door.

CHAPTER 17

LAURA

Monday, October 11, 2010

Loy Porter sat crouched next to a bloodhound petting its head and back. Laura watched as he took the dog's face in both hands and rubbed its jaw, bending forward to kiss it on top of the head.

He looked up at the sound of her car. But instead of greeting their visitor, he turned and trotted into the woods out of sight. The hound at his heels yipped and looked up at him as if wondering why they had to run off.

Laura climbed the porch steps to the front door and looked around. There was an old black Dodge pickup in front of the shed to the right that hadn't been there the day before. But she didn't see or hear anyone else around.

She knocked firmly, remembering Beulah Porter was a bit hard of hearing. Soon she heard a shuffling and the door creaked open. The old woman's face appeared in the crack.

"Good morning, Granny," she ventured. "It's Laura Allen. I visited you with Hattie Perkins yesterday after church and you invited me to come back today. To meet Curry. You remember?"

Beulah Porter looked in Laura's direction, the now familiar hard expression on her face, milky blind eyes not focusing on anything. Laura had to look away. "Aunt Hattie sent some plates of breakfast food. Got it right here in this box. Can I put it in the kitchen for you?"

"S'pose you may as well, since you's here. Just 'bout to make a cup a coffee. Make one for you too if you want." Beulah Porter pulled the door just wide enough for Laura to enter with her burden.

She set the box down on the table as the elderly woman pulled three cups from a cupboard above the pot. Laura emptied the contents of the box onto the table and watched Beulah move around the kitchen with sightless ease.

"Are you hungry for any of this right now? I could warm it up for you," she offered.

"Cur's here. Made us some breakfast couple a hours ago. Just put them plates in the fridge. Top shelf. You be sure an' tell Hattie we're right grateful for 'em." Her grandmother's hard-edged tone didn't match the words she spoke. Beulah finished filling the coffee cups and carried one to the table. Laura followed her lead with the other two. "We don't usually get so many visitors," she stated flatly.

Three visitors in two days was a lot? She got the impression Beulah Porter felt it was too many.

Cream and sugar were on the table along with an old mason jar full of spoons turned up on their ends. Laura was about to ask who the third cup was for when the back door opened.

A tanned leathery man with silver-grey hair entered through the back door and stomped his boots. He looked over at Beulah with a frown before turning away from both of them. Without a word he washed his hands, meticulously folding the towel over the oven handle. This looked like a man who'd always been lean and rugged, and he stood a good head and shoulders taller than Laura.

"Curry, you come on over here and meet your niece, Laura Allen. She come all the way from Pennsylvania to talk to us," Beulah commanded her grown son. "She's Glen's little girl by Robey Foster back in 1960. You 'member?"

He stared at Laura, his gaze filled with suspicion. Curry Porter was in his seventies, his mother in her nineties, but she still ruled the roost in her home. He stepped forward, offering his hand as he looked her in the eye. "I 'member," he nodded.

She took his hand. His taut, sinewy forearms flexed as he gave a brief, too-strong squeeze and released her. The hint of a snarl twitched on his upper lip. Laura couldn't help but stare back. This was her father's brother. The two were close in age. She recognized the similarities.

"I remember you, too," Laura watched his face as she spoke. He was still a strikingly handsome man for his age. "You came with my father to visit sometimes." Laura took a breath and swallowed. "Actually, I came here to ask you about him."

Curry pursed his mouth, brows drawn, and lifted his chin as he spoke, "Cain't tell you nothin'," he replied. "Been gone a long time. Got too much on my mind to worry 'bout the past."

Desperate and tired of running into dead ends, Laura said more than she'd meant to, "I don't mean to bring up painful memories. But . . . the truth is, and I know this sounds crazy, I think he's still alive. I was hoping maybe you'd heard from him. Maybe you could help me find him?"

Curry Porter snarled outright then, "Now you listen' here, young lady. I ain't heard nothin' from Glen. And I'll tell you what else, you ain't heard from him neither." He sneered at her, "Don't know why you'd be comin' back here after all these years pryin' into people's business like you know somethin' we don't. Just 'cause you's kin don't mean you's one of us. Got no right comin' down here upsettin' folks."

Curry Porter had probably just delivered the longest speech he'd made in decades and he'd dumped it all on her.

He grabbed his coffee cup and went out the back door, pulling it shut with a slam. She watched through the window as he disappeared around the corner of the shed. She'd been dismissed without so much as a 'by your leave.' *Hillbilly hell, indeed.* Beulah Porter never said a word.

Laura glanced around as she opened the Jeep door. The black Dodge hadn't moved. She scanned the woods and listened. A lone wolf howled from somewhere not far up the mountain. She shivered.

CHAPTER 18

GLEN

Winter, 1974

Solitude makes for darkness in a man's soul.

Guilt grows and eats at him when he spends most of his time alone.

It took a long time for Glen to convince Curry to bring Loy up to the cabin with him. They argued about it every time he came by. Till one day he showed up at the door with their little brother in tow.

Curry didn't know it, but Loy often visited on his own after that. They sat at the only table in the room and played cards. Or his little brother drew pictures and wrote things for him. Sometimes Glen got him to talk a little, mostly through signals and grunts.

Glen asked him once if Curry was planning something against him. But Loy's eyes got big and he shook his head hard and stared down at the cards.

Then one day, Curry brought Glen new clothes and told him to clean himself up. He couldn't help but wonder what his brother was up to.

Was he about to bring the law up the mountain?

When Glen objected, Curry glared at him. His eyes turned darker, his nostrils flared and he growled, "That's it. We got to get you out of here. Too cold and drafty. You ain't gonna make it another winter. You're movin' to my place. It ain't much, but it's warm. And it's got indoor plumbin'. And I won't have to be comin' all the way up here anymore," Curry grumbled.

Glen stared into his brother's face watching for some sign to convince him this wasn't a trick. He finally gave in. He washed up and changed as Curry gathered and bagged everything from the old Hadley cabin, right down to the bed sheet and blanket.

It was night when Curry came back to get him. He parked the truck down on Porter's Creek Road and they walked out in the dark. But as Glen looked back, a large dark shape with yellow-amber eyes appeared in the cabin doorway.

CHAPTER 19

LAURA

Monday, October 11, 2010

Laura pulled into a parking lot next to an SUV labeled Ashe County Sheriff. The man behind the wheel had the window open partway. She jumped out of the Jeep in a rush to catch him.

"Excuse me, sir, are you the sheriff?" Laura blushed when he turned his gaze on her.

"Why, yes ma'am, I believe so," he joked. He stepped out of the vehicle and extended his hand. "Blaine Wilson. Let me guess," he went on, "you're Laura Allen Porter. I'd be willing to bet my lunch on it."

Laura stammered, "Um, yes. But how did you know?"

The sheriff stepped out of the white Ford and looked down at her. "Oh, we're small-town here. Word gets around—especially when it's about local folks' kin." He smiled as he continued to observe her. "What can I do for you today, ma'am?"

Laura felt her cheeks flush again, "Please, don't call me ma'am. It makes me want to look around for someone—older." She went on, "I'm here to . . . I'm sorry, do you have a few minutes? I don't want to keep you from anything. I could make an appointment." Laura found herself offering to do the exact opposite of what she'd planned.

Blaine Wilson had startling green eyes and his buzz cut blonde hair was flecked with white, along with a touch of grey. She awkwardly craned her neck to look up at him, shading her eyes, squinting against the sun.

He, of course, stood there cool, calm and collected.

"Not necessary, ma'am." The hint of a grin lifted the corner of his mouth, "I mean, Miss Porter. Come on in the office." The sheriff gestured toward the brick, three-story building behind him.

It was an imposing structure fronted by wide cement steps leading up to a covered porch expanse with tan columns, *ASHE COUNTY LAW ENFORCEMENT CENTER* printed in contrasting brown at the top. She was impressed with the dignified, professional looking, "small-town" Sheriff's office.

Laura followed the man inside. He spoke to a few people along the way, another officer, a receptionist, a dispatcher, and then led her into a neatly ordered office where he offered her a chair and a cup of coffee. She accepted both. It seemed everything this man did, he did with calm efficiency, right down to folding his large muscular frame behind that beautiful mahogany desk.

Laura glanced at the wall and shelves behind him as he sat down. Photos showed Sheriff Wilson kneeling next to a large buck holding the head up by the antlers. A few appeared to be onsite at a military camp of some kind. He stood with several other men— all in BDUs. Some cradled guns in their arms like babies, the sheriff included. *Enough,* she scolded herself. She was here to get his professional help, not his life story.

"Now then, what would you like to talk about, Miss Porter?" the sheriff asked.

She shifted in her seat and glanced down before she spoke. "Please feel free to call me Laura," she told him. Then she pulled the hand-scrawled note out of her pocket, unfolded it, and laid it on top of his desk. "I'm here because I want to find out what happened to my father, Glen Porter. And I think I got *that*," she pointed to the paper, "because someone doesn't want me to." She avoided telling him about the phone calls that actually brought her here.

The sheriff picked up the piece of paper and looked at it several seconds. "Hmm." He raised both eyebrows and tilted his head as he continued to study it. "Where and when did you find this?" The man carried the calm demeanor to the extreme.

Laura explained about her hike. She didn't mention the screaming girl—she didn't want him to write her off as a completely hysterical female. But she did tell him she thought there was someone in the woods behind the cabin.

Sheriff Wilson frowned at that. "Could have been someone else hiking. Or hunters." His brow creased further. "Alright then," he seemed to have settled on a decision. "I'll keep this note. And I'll go out there and have a look around." Sheriff Wilson pulled out a small, top-bound spiral notepad and jotted something down.

"Sheriff?"

"Yes, Miss Laura?"

She hesitated, "I know you're bound by the law, but you lived here in 1967 when my father disappeared."

He nodded but didn't say anything.

Laura continued, "Your father was sheriff back then. Do you know anything about what happened? He is my father. I have a right to know."

Sheriff Wilson stopped as though searching his memory. "That was a long time ago." *Deciding how much to reveal perhaps?* "My dad didn't talk much about his work around me."

He looked down at his notes and tapped the tablet with his pen.

"I'll tell you what. Let me take some time this afternoon to pull the records and refresh my memory. Then I'll stop by your aunt's and give you what I can after I check out the Dillon place. That sound good to you?"

Laura decided not to mention Carl Edwards. "I have some things I want to do in town before I head back. Could you make it later? I should be back at my aunt's by four or five o'clock."

Blaine Wilson rose from his chair and stepped around the desk in front of her before she had the chance to get up. "I'll plan on going out there last thing today then."

His sudden proximity made her feel small. Standing up herself didn't do much to alleviate the sensation. He reached for her elbow as she rose. She glanced up at him and drew in a breath, conscious he may have heard it. Her face warmed in spite of herself. But he escorted her back through the building like a true southern gentleman.

"Thank you, Sheriff. I appreciate you taking the time to look into all of this." She deliberately averted her gaze as she spoke.

"Yes, ma'am, not a problem. In the meantime, maybe you should stay out of the woods for now. At least, don't go out alone. Err on the side of caution. It's usually best," he advised.

"Yes, sir," she replied obediently. She noted he'd gone back to the formal use of 'ma'am' with her in front of other people.

He offered his hand again. Was she imagining it or did he hold on a bit longer than necessary?

He pushed the door open for her then, causing her to have to duck under his arm. Laura felt a sudden wave of nostalgia at the scent of his cologne. She missed the smell of a man. She climbed back into the Jeep, stunned by her own reaction.

As she glanced back up at the building she saw him in the portico. He gave her a crooked, masculine smile and a mini salute with the first two fingers of his right hand. She waved and backed out of her parking spot—feeling acutely self-conscious.

CHAPTER 20

GLEN

Wednesday, September 1, 2010

Glen was bed-ridden for a week with the flu. He coughed till he couldn't breathe and his whole body burned with fever. He wondered if he would make it through this illness.

When he was finally able to get out of bed and keep food down, he decided the time had come to contact his little girl. She was his only hope of redemption, the one good thing he would leave behind when he died.

Glen had been in hiding over forty years now. He thought he was about seventy years old, but he couldn't remember exactly. He figured he didn't have too many years left on this earth. He had to reach out to his little girl before it was too late.

It'd be risky, but he'd get Loy to help. Though it'd be hard to convince his brother it was for the good.

Glen bided his time. Then he slipped out one night when Curry was away on a job. It was late, but he found Loy in the living room in front of the TV. His little brother was startled at first. Glen had to coax him outside. Their Momma was in bed, sure would be nice to see her, but the chance for that had long passed.

Glen wasn't sure Loy understood what he wanted, but his brother spent a lot of time at the library and had learned how to use computers. He told him to hide the note under a rock by the base of the old triple tree up on Pond Road.

And that's where Glen found the printed page with a name, address and phone number for his Laurie Allen. At least he hoped it was. The name written at the top was Laura Evans. But a hand printed note along the side read, "THIS BE HER."

Glen tucked it away in his shirt and headed home. There was no phone in the trailer so he waited again. He folded and unfolded the paper so many times it got thin in the creases before another chance came for him to sneak out. It was time his little girl knew the truth about her daddy . . . whatever the consequences.

CHAPTER 21

LAURA

Monday, October 11, 2010

Laura hadn't told Sheriff Wilson what her plans were for the rest of the afternoon. She was afraid he would tell her not to investigate on her own. Right or wrong, she didn't want to hear it.

Carl Edwards' home was a small one-story brick house with a covered car port. Laura knocked firmly on the side door. If this was the Carl Edwards she sought, he'd be in his early eighties. An elderly man moved the curtain aside and peeked out. Laura smiled warmly to set his mind at ease. He opened the inside door and peered out through the screen.

"Yes, ma'am?" he greeted her tentatively.

"Hello, Mr. Edwards. My name is Laura Evans. I don't mean to disturb you, but are you the Carl Edwards who lived in the Porter's Hollow area back in the '60s?"

He hesitated, "Yes ma'am, me and my wife . . . and our little girl. What'd you say your name was?"

"Laura Evans, but my last name used to be Porter. Glen Porter was my father. I was hoping I could talk with you a few minutes."

"I 'member you," he said as he pointed at Laura. "You're the one found my Lottie. What in heaven's name brings you back here?"

"I'd like to explain, if you have time."

"I don't get visitors much. Place is a mess," he pushed the screen door open.

Carl Edwards wasn't much taller than Laura. His back was humped and he shuffled slowly as he led her across a tiny kitchen to the living room beyond. He pointed to an old sofa with a faded blue afghan stretched across the back. Then he took a seat in a grey recliner worn smooth with his shape.

"Mr. Edwards," Laura paused, not sure how to begin. "I'm here in North Carolina because I think my father may still be alive."

She watched the man's face as she spoke, surprised at his expression. He nodded with his whole upper body, lips pursed. "Yes, ma'am, I tried to tell the sheriff that years ago. But nobody wanted to hear it, not from me."

"I'm confused. You mean *you* think he's alive, too?"

The old man nodded again, "Yes'm. But why don't you tell me why you think so."

Laura took a breath and sighed before she spoke, "Because I got a phone call from him. He said he wanted to explain things to me, but he also said there was someone else who probably wouldn't let him." She paused to give the elderly man time to take in what she said. "But, I actually came here to ask you about your little girl. It was right after I found her that my father disappeared. I know the police investigated both incidents, but I was told they never found anything connecting them."

Carl Edwards' voice was sharp, but tears formed in the corners of his wrinkled eyes. "My little girl was killed, and hid there under that porch so's nobody'd ever find her. That's what happened. Nobody found no evidence, 'cause after all those years, there weren't none left. I got my ideas. But I'm not sure you want to hear what I have to say." He sunk down in his chair, a tired and weary look on his face.

"No, please go on. I've come this far," she encouraged him.

The tears pooling at the corners of his eyes spilled out and ran down his weathered cheeks as he spoke, "Well, like I told the sheriff back then, somebody had to draw my Lottie out that night. She'd gone to bed. I'd seen her off and shut her door myself. It woulda had to be somebody she knew, and trusted."

The elderly man pulled a handkerchief out of his back pocket and wiped his eyes.

"My wife and me, we never heard nothin' in the night. But come mornin' I called for Lottie. She usually jumped right up and come out to hug me. Not that mornin'. I went to her room to see if she was ailin' or somethin'. But she was gone. Seven years later, you crawl up under that porch and . . . She musta been there the whole time. She was only fourteen—fourteen. And innocent as a babe, 'cause she had that Down Syndrome." Carl Edwards sighed and sagged deeper into his chair.

He closed his eyes and dropped his chin forward. Laura thought he'd nodded off to sleep. But then he shook his head and breathed deep.

Suddenly he went on, "I shouldn't a gone along with Mamie's plan. Never shoulda taken my little girl down to Raleigh for that op'ration. It was God's judgment, that's what it was. It wasn't a month later she disappeared forever."

Carl Edwards practically jumped up and left the room. She could hear a door open and he shuffled around a bit before it got quiet again. She was about to call out to him when he came back with a thick folder he handed to her. Then he lowered himself back into the recliner.

"That there explains it all. That's the paperwork they give me at the hospital, and them's the pamphlets Mamie had. And the other stuff, it's all 'bout what I found out later 'bout somethin' they called U-genics. It was a evil plan, that's what it was. A evil plan to eliminate people like my Lottie Mae. Innocent, helpless, simple-minded folks who don't know no evil themselves. And all 'cause they was different."

He sighed and shook his head.

"It was God's judgment. Sure enough. An' it was all my fault." Carl Edwards looked at Laura, his eyes begging her to explain the hardness of life.

She had no answers for him.

"Mr. Edwards, I'm so sorry about your little girl. But I'm sure none of it was your fault. It sounds like you were a good father. You can't blame yourself for what happened," Laura paused, not sure what to say to ease the poor man's suffering. "Do you mind if I borrow this?" she asked lifting the folder. "I'll bring it back to you before I leave North Carolina. And I can give you my cell phone number if you want."

Carl Edwards raised his gaze to her face again, "You can have that stuff. I don't need it no more. Ain't nothin' else I can do 'bout it. I'll see you to the door, ma'am." The old man's shoulders drooped as he led her out.

The afternoon had waned as they visited and it was nearing 4:00 p.m. She pulled into a 7-Eleven to grab a drink and give Aunt Hattie a call.

Laura opened the folder Carl Edwards had given her to have a quick look through it as she sat in the parking lot. There was a small pamphlet on sterilization with diagrams, and a brief explanation of the process along with a doctor's name and number.

Laura set this aside and picked up a copy of a medical consent form. It had obviously been filled out for Lottie Edwards and signed by her mother and father. The faded date read August 10, 1960. The rest of the pile was made up of printouts from websites on Eugenics.

She had to admit she was a little surprised to see a computer and printer on the desk in Carl Edwards' living room. He must have searched all this stuff on his own.

Sad, she thought. *Sick even*, but Lottie's sterilization had been a voluntary decision made by her parents. Mostly her mother, according to Mr. Edwards. But the idea of eliminating people with defects or disabilities by limiting those allowed to breed was a policy protected and promoted by law back then.

It began here in the United States years before Hitler's idea of breeding for a superior Aryan race. And it continued to be legal in many states years after the end of the second world war. Laura had even heard about recent cases of forced sterilization of some prisoners.

But Carl Edwards was convinced Lottie had been abducted and killed as a direct judgment God had visited upon him for what they had done to her. The man had been punishing himself for it all these years.

Laura couldn't bring herself to believe that any God would bring that kind of punishment on the innocent. If there was any fault involved it wasn't Lottie's, so how could God sentence her to pain, suffering, and death for something she had no choice in? Yet, she couldn't escape the nagging feeling the sterilization had something to do with what happened to the girl.

She started to push all the paperwork together and shove it back into the folder when one piece slipped out. Laura retrieved it as it floated onto the passenger seat.

It was an old newspaper article titled, "Local Child Goes Missing from Home." And there was a photo of Lottie Edwards. The picture was faded and crinkled but . . . Laura caught her breath, it was definitely the child from her nightmares.

She shoved everything back in the folder then. If there was any connection between her father and Lottie's disappearance, it wasn't likely to be found there. *But,* the thought finally formed clearly in her mind, *it was somehow being communicated to her personally.*

When she left the 7-Eleven a few minutes later, an old black Dodge pickup spun its tires as it pulled out ahead of her.

CHAPTER 22

GLEN

Saturday, October 2, 2010

Glen held his breath in the quiet darkness. His heart thumped so heavy his body rocked in rhythm to it.

He held in a cough. Fought it back so hard he nearly passed out.

There was a pay phone on the corner of the 7-Eleven parking lot. It wasn't more than fifty yards away from where he hid behind a trash dumpster. But Glen hadn't been near town in years. He didn't want to see anybody, or be seen. He'd hoped the place would be empty this time of night. So again, he waited.

By the time the single car near the door pulled away, he was feeling weak, and breathless. But he had to make this call.

He ended up doing it over a couple times 'cause of the damned hacking fits. When the phone finally cut out on him with that screeching sound, he was exhausted. But he was satisfied he'd gotten his message through to the right person.

He pushed the booth door open and stood for a minute. His neck prickled. He felt eyes on him. But the place was deserted as far as he could see.

Glen rounded the dumpster and entered the cover of the woods again, breathing easier. He didn't think anybody had seen him. He still had plenty of time to make it back home before Curry got there.

CHAPTER 23

LAURA

Monday, October 11, 2010

Blaine Wilson's black and white SUV sat in Hattie Perkins' driveway when Laura got back from Jefferson. She was so preoccupied she'd forgot he was supposed to stop by. Nerves did a dance in the pit of her stomach as she climbed the porch steps.

Aunt Hattie called to her, "Come on out to the kitchen, Laura. We got company."

She walked into the room to find the sheriff sampling a pot of something on the stove. He cradled one huge paw under a ladle, blowing on the contents. Then he devoured the whole spoonful in one bite. "Mmm, that's the best chicken gumbo I ever tasted. I believe I'll take you up on that offer." He turned his full attention on Hattie Perkins as he spoke.

Laura's stomach did a flip. *He's staying for dinner?*

She busied herself helping her aunt set out the food. At supper, Blaine Wilson carried the conversation, checking on Hattie's arthritis, asking Laura about herself, describing the area, its history. *He fits here. Part of the rugged countryside like the woods, the mountain, the hollow.*

Hattie turned to Blaine, "You can tell Laura was born here. She loves these mountains. Maybe you could show her around some? Help refresh her memory."

Laura's face warmed and she refused to look at him when she spoke, "I'm sure the sheriff is too busy to play tour guide." She chanced a sideways glance at him then.

Blaine Wilson's voice sounded uneasy. "I'm sure I could make some time." He paused. "For now, it's probably best if she stays out of the woods. At least till I figure out if there's anything to this note she got." He tilted his head, one eyebrow raised, and their eyes met.

Everyone pitched in to clear the table, but the sheriff insisted on doing the dishes. Laura grabbed a towel determined to do her part, and to keep her hands, and her mind busy.

"Looks like you two have this under control. Think I'll catch the evenin' news." Aunt Hattie didn't wait for a response. She headed into the sitting room without a backward glance. Laura felt herself blush again.

"So, Miss Laura, what did you find out today?"

"Hmm?" she murmured, still rattled by her aunt's cupid role.

"Your afternoon," he added. "How'd your plans go after you left my office? I had the impression you were on a mission."

She stopped drying the plate she held and looked up at him. "I found an address for Lottie Edwards' father, so I went to see him. I hoped he could tell me more."

He shook his head and frowned. "I could've told you where he was myself. Probably could have saved you the trip if you'd asked me."

Blaine Wilson rinsed the pot he'd just washed and set it in the dish drainer. Then he turned toward her, gazing into her face, studying her. "I am a law enforcement officer," he sighed. "I know we're pretty simple folk down here, and we may seem a little informal, but that doesn't mean we're unprofessional—or deceitful."

He handed her a plate and continued, "I like to think it's just the opposite. I care about the people in my jurisdiction personally. Your Aunt Hattie is a friend and a citizen of this county. If she was in danger, I'd be here for her in both capacities."

He paused until she looked up. "I'd like you to see me that way, too. I'll share with you what I can. There are some professional limitations. But most of it is public record, or non-privileged information anyway."

He paused as he watched her face. Then he tilted his head and took the last dish from her hands, putting it in the cupboard above her. "Why don't you tell me what's been going on first? Then I'll fill in the blanks for you where I can."

Laura retrieved the folder Carl Edwards had given her and laid it out on the table. He looked at her and raised one eyebrow. They both sat down and he leafed through the papers.

She commented as she watched his face, "That little girl disappeared on the night I was born. Seven years later I was the one to find her body—what was left of it. Less than two weeks later my father disappeared, and days after that my mother packed us up and we left town."

Laura told him then about the phone calls and how she fully believed they were from her father. She decided to tell him about the screams she'd heard by the cabin also. And since she was on a roll, she told him she suspected Curry Porter might be following her.

Blaine Wilson regarded her with a look of concentration as she talked, but at the mention of her suspicions about Curry, he frowned. Heavy brows shadowed his deep green eyes.

"Hmm." He sat his coffee cup down and leaned forward in his chair, both elbows propped on the table. "I checked the records. The girl's skull had been damaged. But without any other physical evidence, there just wasn't much that could be done. Especially after that long." The sheriff sat back again. "It was the 60s. Technology was lacking. And I'm afraid some cases didn't get the attention they deserved. This one got turned over to detectives in Charlotte because it was a possible kidnapping and homicide. But when they didn't turn anything up after more than a month . . ." Blaine let the sentence hang as he shrugged one shoulder and made an apologetic face.

Laura shook her head and sighed.

The sheriff flipped his notepad open and went on, "One detective concluded, quote, *Carlotta Mae Edwards wandered off on her own in the night, fell and hit her head on a rock, and managed to crawl up under the cabin porch to get warm, where she died of a combination of head trauma and exposure.*"

The sheriff pulled out two small, top-bound spiral notebooks like the one he carried.

"But, that was the official record. My father kept his own notes. I stopped by the house on my way out here and dug through them. He mostly put things in here that were his impressions. Things he thought but had no real evidence for. This one's dated September 1 through September 30, 1960. Back when Lottie Edwards first disappeared."

He flipped it open and began to read, " '*Had a talk with the Porter boys 'cause someone said they'd seen them heading toward the hollow earlier yesterday evening, on their way home. Good old country boys, just trying to make a living, most likely. Get a little rowdy now and then, but kidnapping? I don't know.*' " The sheriff flipped ahead in the notebook. "But then a few pages later he says, '*I can't put my finger on it. Something's just not adding up about those Porter boys.*' There's not much else though. Just says he'll have to keep his eyes and ears open around them."

Laura propped an elbow on the table, resting her chin on the heel of her hand, eyebrows drawn in concentration as the sheriff read.

"But this one," he picked up another notepad, "this one's dated October 1 through October 30, 1967." Blaine flipped to the page he wanted and read aloud, " '*Downright awful that little Porter girl had to find those bones. Poor thing was pale as a ghost when I talked to her.*' " He skipped a page and went on, " '*Something about those Porter boys just don't set right with me. Detectives cleared them, so there ain't much I can do. It's just a feeling I got. Glen Porter disappears, Loy can't talk at all, and Curry claims he don't remember nothing.*' And that's it. He doesn't even mention them again."

Laura frowned and sighed. There had to be a clue in all this somewhere.

The sheriff watched her, his expression unreadable. "I think I can guess what Carl Edwards had to say about it," he added a moment later.

Laura looked up at him tentatively before responding. "He said Lottie wouldn't have wandered away on her own. And she wouldn't have gone with a stranger. He claimed he went to see the sheriff and the detectives back then and told them he thought my dad was alive and hiding out somewhere." Laura leaned in toward the sheriff as she looked at the tiny booklet in his sizable, rugged hands. "Does your father mention anything about that in his notebooks?"

Blaine Wilson followed her glance and she looked away self-consciously.

He cleared his throat and took a sip of his coffee before he spoke. "Like I said, nothing much more in there. But then it wasn't long after, my dad had his first heart attack. He was only thirty-five at the time. His deputy had to function without him for a while. The case had been dropped by the detectives in Charlotte by the time he got back to work. And my father had to move on."

The sheriff looked away from her then. He appeared to be lost in thought as he studied a spot on the table.

He broke the silence with a question she feared would make her seem foolish, no matter how she answered it. "But you said something else a few minutes ago. About hearing screams or cries of some kind out by the old Dillon place. Can you describe the sound?"

"It was at the back corner of the cabin where I'd found Lottie Edwards' bones."

Laura noted the sheriff's body language before she continued. He still sat back in his chair, one shoulder higher than the other.

He set his coffee cup on the table and propped his clasped hands on his upper thigh.

She breathed deep and continued, "It sounded like a little girl's voice crying, *why*. I know how that must sound to you, but I can only tell you what I heard. And it was close, very close."

Blaine lifted both eyebrows briefly and tilted his head in thought. "Bobcat maybe. Or a barn cat wandering around." The corner of his mouth lifted in the hint of a grin. "When I was a kid, we had an old yellow tabby used to howl like that whenever she was in heat. Could've sworn there was some old witch in the shed cooking up a brew. Good mouser though, good momma too. Nursed all the stray kittens."

The sheriff didn't believe her. Laura heard those screams, it was no cat. He would think she was crazy if she claimed Lottie Edwards was trying to communicate with her.

And she'd been ready to tell him about the dreams, too. *No point.*

The sheriff broke into her thoughts, "I went out there and scouted around. Didn't find anything conclusive. Some prints, human and animal, could've been made anytime. Some probably yours. Hard to say." Blaine Wilson straightened in his chair, a 'this sheriff means business' look in his eyes. "I'll have a talk with Curry Porter. See if I can get anything out of Loy. Hard to believe your father is still alive in hiding somewhere. But if he is, I'll find him, and get to the bottom of this once and for all."

Then he leveled his gaze at her. "I want you to hold off on this search of yours for now. Let me do some more poking around. I'll let you know what I find."

He was a persuasive man, and he was the sheriff. But she refused to be put off focus. He couldn't force her to abandon her efforts legally.

"Sheriff, I appreciate everything you're doing, but I've waited over forty years to find out the truth about my father. And I came all the way down here myself to do just that."

He sighed, "I guess I can't stop you, long as you aren't doing anything illegal. But if you come across anything . . ." he wrote his number on a napkin and handed it to her. "And stay away from Curry Porter. He's not known for his charitable disposition."

"Thank you, Sheriff. I really do appreciate your help."

"It's my job," he replied. "Don't suppose you've got a cell phone number you can give me for future reference?" he asked as he pulled his notepad out of his pocket and averted his gaze.

Laura felt the heat rise in her cheeks. She had to think a moment before she could respond. She finally came up with it but not till shortly after the silence got downright embarrassing.

Blaine Wilson stood and stretched his neck. He picked up his coffee cup, finished off its contents and put the mug in the sink. Laura rose and did the same.

The sheriff turned toward the sitting room, but Hattie Perkins had fallen asleep in her chair. He looked back at Laura, put a finger to his lips and grinned. Then he held out his hand. His touch made her face go warm again. She was glad for the dim porch light.

At the bottom of the steps he looked back and smiled as he tipped his hat and gave her the two-fingered salute, softly adding, " 'Night, Miss Laura."

Her stomach did a somersault, but she smiled and waved.

CHAPTER 24

CURRY

Saturday, October 2, 2010

Leave it to a woman to be their undoing after all these years.

Glen never had been too smart when it came to women. Now he'd gone and called that girl of his to come here. And he'd never seen Curry watching from the alley across the street.

Glen was a fool. Women were his soft spot like that Achilles fella's heel.

Not him. Curry knew what women were for and what they wanted. Always turning their big wet eyes on a man, trying to wear him down and take his whole soul. They always wanted more of a man than he wanted to give. Whether it was money, clothes, a home, babies, it didn't matter. They got in a man's head through his eyes first. They'd show him wonderful things, then they'd take him for a ride he'd never forget.

"C'mon, Curry. Let's go out to the pond for a swim, Curry."

"You can look but don't touch, Curry."

"You didn't really think I'd ever let you have me that way did you, Curry?"

Well, he'd showed them plenty hisself. Women learned not to mess with Curvin Henry Porter. And with Glen hidden away and Loy too dumb to understand anything, he'd been able to supply the beast with as many as he needed.

But now that girl his brother sired knew he was alive. And it was for sure she'd be coming back to look for her daddy.

Well, that was fine then. Let her come. If she turned her eyes on him, he'd be ready.

CHAPTER 25

LAURA

Tuesday, October 12, 2010

The preacher stepped out from the garage when Laura pulled in the driveway. He shielded his eyes from the afternoon sun with one hand and waved with the other. As Laura turned the car off, he opened Aunt Hattie's door to help her out. "Hello there, ladies. Nice to see you two this fine afternoon. Glad you could make it."

"Well, thank you, Reverend." Hattie took his proffered hand and he guided them through the garage by a side entrance into the living room.

"Can I get you ladies something to drink? We've got coffee, iced tea, water, pop."

"Oh, I think I'll have a glass of Lizabeth's sweet tea," her aunt declared.

Laura was taken back by the sense of familiarity. She felt like she was on uneven ground, out of place, even with Aunt Hattie. She had the uncomfortable, and somehow sad feeling she didn't belong.

"Hey, sweetie, this here's Laura Evans. Laura, this is my wife, Elizabeth," the preacher introduced them as the other woman entered the room.

"It's so good to meet you. I'm sorry I didn't get to church the other day. Tom's told me so much about you, I already feel I know you." She smiled, and the way the skin at the corners of her warm blue eyes crinkled in her sun-kissed face put Laura at ease. But she wondered why the woman called her husband Tom—not Cecil.

And how could he have told his wife all about her? He didn't know that much himself, did he?

"Miss Hattie, it's been a while since you came for dinner. I'm so glad you could both make it." Elizabeth Honeywell hugged the older woman.

They talked about Aunt Hattie's arthritis, the new piano at the church and the old piano player, who had died lately and who had given birth, whether it had been a boy or a girl, and so on. Then the conversation turned to Laura, where she lived, was she married, did she have any children. How did she like Pennsylvania? In spite of her suspicions she found herself responding openly to this couple's genuine friendliness.

They continued the give-and-take over dinner. Then Elizabeth asked Aunt Hattie to help her clear the table. She nodded to her husband, "Tom, you go ahead and take Laura into the living room. I think it's time you two had a little chat on your own."

Laura looked up as Elizabeth leaned across the table to pick up the serving plate of leftover pot roast. The expression on her face insinuated it was time her husband took care of business. Cecil Honeywell dropped his gaze to the floor for a few seconds. Then with a sigh of resignation he slapped the tops of both thighs and stood.

"Miss Laura, would you join me in the living room, please? There's something we need to talk about."

Laura looked from him to Aunt Hattie, and then to Elizabeth again. The look on Hattie Perkins' face gave Laura the impression she knew exactly what this was all about.

Laura followed the preacher into the living room without comment where he reached for a large vinyl-covered photo album and motioned for her to sit on the sofa. He flipped open the cover and slid the book across for her to hold. There were several black and white pictures of a baby. Some were in the arms of a woman who was apparently his mother. They had tiny hand-written, faded white labels glued below them.

Some were of other people, but the woman and the growing boy recurred frequently as she turned the pages. The baby name below the first picture read *Cecil Thomas Honeywell, born July 13, 1956, Shatley Springs, NC.*

So the reverend had been born right here in North Carolina. That explained the southern accent. But she still didn't understand why she needed to know this, until she turned the next page. The picture in the top left corner was of the same young boy, a toddler then, seated on the lap of a man she recognized instantly. The faded label read *Tommy Honeywell and Glen Porter, August 1, 1959.*

Laura glanced up at the preacher. "I don't understand," she stammered.

But even as she said it, she knew. His dark hair and blue-grey eyes, the twinkle in them when he smiled, his height and build—Glen Porter was this man's father. And that meant Cecil Thomas Honeywell, the preacher, was her brother.

"I wasn't sure how, or even *if,* I should tell you. Your Aunt Hattie thought you should know. Lizabeth too. They ganged up on me. I just didn't think—I didn't know if you'd even want to know. Your—our—daddy, was only sixteen when I was born. My momma too. They were young and foolish, but the truth was they were never really in love. But he did his best to help support me for my momma's sake. He'd come by and visit often, right up till the day he disappeared."

Laura stared at him speechless as he continued.

"I was four years old when he met your momma. Robey knew about me, but she didn't seem to mind. Those two were in love," he added emphatically.

"But Callie Parker had taken a likin' to him and she got him in trouble with her daddy so he'd have to marry her. He said she came on to him, tried to get him to—well—you know. Claimed he didn't remember doin' anythin' like that with her, but he'd been drinkin'."

Laura looked at this man telling her things about her own parents she'd never known, and all she could do was shake her head. "My mother knew about you? And she never told me? Why? And Aunt Hattie? *She knew?*"

Tom sighed and nodded, "Yes. But Hattie didn't tell you back then because your momma wouldn't let her. She called and told me you were comin' to visit and asked whether I thought you should know now. I asked her to wait till I had the chance to talk to you myself."

He leaned forward, placing his elbow on his knee.

"As to why your momma never wanted you to know? I'm guessing she just didn't want any ties to this place once she got out of here. I can't really blame her. In a lot of ways, I did the same thing for years." The preacher returned her steady gaze.

Laura watched his face, remembering her father's features. He had to be telling the truth, but suddenly he averted his eyes. She suspected there was more.

"What about the other child? And Callie Parker?"

He looked up. "There was no other child. Callie was never pregnant. She just wanted to get away from her daddy. But the year after Glen disappeared, she hanged herself in the shed out back of Beulah's."

"And Aunt Hattie knew about all this and still never told me?" she bristled.

"Don't be angry with Aunt Hattie. She was only trying to honor everyone's wishes. Poor woman's had a lot of years of holding other people's secrets, and feeling like she was betraying the truth, betraying her God, betraying you by doing it too," he finished sadly.

Laura sighed and dropped her gaze back to the album. She continued to leaf through its pages without a word. She shook her head in wonder, emotions churning inside.

The minister pointed out a few photos as she turned the pages. Telling her where they were taken, who some of the other people were and how they were related. As he talked she realized he must have spent a lot more time with their father than she ever had the opportunity to. But she wondered when, and how. He was a few years older than her but he would still have been a young child when Glen Porter disappeared.

Laura looked up at him, silent for several seconds as she did the math.

"I'm confused. How old were you when he disappeared? Eleven, twelve maybe? Seems like a lot of personal stuff for a man to share with such a young child—even if you are his own son."

Tom Honeywell sighed and sat back into the corner of the sofa. He propped his elbow on the arm of the couch and tilted his head. He seemed to study her face a long moment before he spoke.

"You're right. I was thirteen at the time. But the truth is," and he hesitated before continuing, "he didn't disappear—well, not really. He went into hiding."

He continued to watch her face as she took in that disconcerting little piece of information.

"What?" Laura's mouth dropped open. "Why? And you didn't let on when you met me Sunday morning?" A sense of betrayal made a fist in her stomach.

Tom gave an affirmative shoulder shrug.

"And he *is* still alive, then? Where is he?" Laura's voice took on a bitter edge. She couldn't believe he had let her think he wanted to help when he already knew what had happened to their father.

"Whoa, wait a minute. I knew where he was, *back then*. I don't know if he's still alive now, or where he'd be hiding if he is." He spread both hands in a cross-out motion.

"But you've been back here several years. And you haven't seen or heard from him?" Laura raised one eyebrow and stared hard at her half-brother.

"No, I haven't. Not long after I moved back here, I went to the old cabin where he'd been living when I left. But it was deserted. I kept hoping if he was still around, he'd hear I was back and contact me. But there may be a very good reason why he wouldn't."

Laura sought Tom's face. *Would the secrets never end?*

He sighed again, "I'm a minister now." He announced it as if that explained it all. When she didn't catch on he continued, "I left here at seventeen, disillusioned and disgusted with life, and with him. I ended up in Maryland where I got a decent job, and eventually found myself in a church where I met Elizabeth. After we married, we decided it was a calling for us, so we went to seminary. That's how I ended up a Baptist minister."

Laura shook her head and made a face. Where was he going with this?

"Our father went into hiding all those years ago out of guilt and shame. And because he believed himself to be possessed, tormented by whatever attacked them on the road that night. At least that's what he said. He called it 'the beast' and claimed it owned his soul and he would never be free. He said he'd take his sin and guilt to the grave one day. He believed he was doomed to hell."

Tom sighed heavily then. "He never actually told me what exactly he thought he was guilty of. But I was young, and I didn't want to be the one to get my own father in any kind of trouble."

Laura couldn't believe what she'd heard. Here she sat with someone, a brother she never knew she had, who had seen and visited with her father—their father—for years after he'd gone missing.

"Where is this cabin? I need to know," Laura said at last.

He appeared to contemplate the question a moment. "It's the old Hadley cabin. Up over the mountain from your Aunt Hattie's. They never wanted a path kept open to it back then. Always had to scramble through brush, and never the same way twice."

Laura sat back and trained her eyes on her brother's face, crossing her arms.

"But it's even worse now. It wouldn't be safe for you to go traipsing around up there," Tom warned. "Besides, there was never any phone service out there. He couldn't have called you from that place."

Laura hit the same wall again. It seemed no one down here wanted her to find Glen Porter. And she still wasn't sure of her newfound brother's loyalties.

At that moment, Aunt Hattie and the preacher's wife entered the room.

"My goodness, would you look at the time," Aunt Hattie started right in as if Tom Honeywell hadn't just revealed the most startling news Laura ever heard. "It's after seven. It'll be my bedtime till we get home. You ready, Laura?"

Laura shook her head again, trying to clear her mind. "Yes, ma'am. I guess we'd better be going." She turned to Elizabeth then, "I'm sorry, I didn't mean to ignore you. I'm just a little overwhelmed."

"That's okay. It's perfectly understandable. We'll visit more another time. Often, I hope." Elizabeth hugged Laura.

Aunt Hattie locked an arm into the crook of Laura's elbow as they walked out. The minister and his wife followed. They waved goodbye as Laura backed the car out of the drive, her mind still swirling.

The two women rode along without speaking for several minutes. It was Aunt Hattie who finally broke the silence. "I'm real sorry I couldn't tell you all this years ago," she sighed. "It was a sad time, so many folks hurtin' over things. But I felt I had to honor your momma's wishes while you were young."

Laura's eyes glistened with unshed tears. The dam was about to overflow. She swallowed hard and forced them open wider, blinking fast before she spoke again.

"It's all right. I understand completely. My mother was always secretive about her life here. That's not your fault."

As they entered the house, Aunt Hattie reached out and patted Laura's arm, then she turned to hug her niece. Laura responded with a gentle squeeze, but the floodgate was about to open and she needed to be alone. It would be the first time she'd cried since before Doug died—it was all coming to a head at once.

She fell asleep, at last, tears still damp on her pillow. And still unable to decide what was sadder—the hollow emptiness of her relationships with her mother and her husband, being denied a relationship with her own brother for years, or the tragic desperation of her real father's life.

Somehow, in a strange disjointed way, she felt responsible for them all.

CHAPTER 26

GLEN

Monday, October 11, 2010

He couldn't believe it. His little girl was here in Grassy Creek. Loy managed to communicate it to him in his broken mix of words, pictures and signals.

Glen needed to set up a meeting. He'd have to wait for the right opportunity. But he wanted to let her know he knew she was here. Wrote the note himself and gave it to Loy.

He couldn't tell her where he was. He didn't want her to come out here to the trailer. They couldn't risk it. Curry could show up, and he might not be alone. And who knew what would happen then?

CHAPTER 27

LAURA

Wednesday, October 13, 2010

Laura woke with a cringing headache, red eyes and a puffy face. She hated that face.

Why did people always talk about a 'good cry' like all you had to do to feel fine again was to shed tears in greater quantity? But Laura knew she'd bottled up too much emotion far too long.

A splash of cold water and a cup of Hattie's strong, black coffee were in order. And a few pain relievers, after she ate a little something.

It didn't help that her sleep continued to be interrupted by dreams of the girl she now knew to be Lottie Edwards. This time, the child stood off at a distance in a dark woods motioning to her to come.

Laura could see her face clearly in spite of the distance. The unmistakable slanted eyes and slightly pudgy features. Her skin milky white, her pale blue dress luminescent in the moonlight.

Then came the dark creature. It snarled and growled as it swelled to twice its size before her eyes. She watched it approach Lottie, but the little girl didn't move. She stood frozen to the spot. Her eyes pleading silently for help.

At breakfast Laura picked at the eggs on her plate, her stomach unsettled by the severe headache. She opted for toast and one piece of sausage, and nursed the coffee along for the caffeine. She sat with both hands on her cup, her gaze directed at the dark shiny surface.

"Aunt Hattie?" Laura began but paused. She didn't think the older woman overheard her conversation with the preacher. She decided to venture a few questions. "Do you know anything about an old place around here they call the Hadley cabin?"

The older woman nodded, "You mean old Rube Hadley's. Story was some boys went walkin' up through there huntin' one day and found her body hangin' from the porch rafters." Laura's eyebrows rose as Hattie went on. "The cabin was near the top of the mountain, as I recall. Up the dirt lane to the left off Porter's Creek Road."

Aunt Hattie paused and stared off across the room, her lips pursed.

Then her gaze refocused on Laura. "The other road to the right up the hollow used to run back up around the mountain this way. It came right down to meet the lane by the Dillon's cabin." She motioned with one hand. "It was called Pond Hill Road 'cause there was a spring-fed pond in the woods up there. It's a few miles, mind you, but it all connected back then."

"Really? How many miles would you say it was?" Laura sat forward on the edge of her seat.

"Not right sure, but your momma used to walk it all the time. Doc's house was back there too, and the Edwards' family. Most of the places got left empty. No kin to inherit them, I guess." Hattie looked as if she thought that was a sad state of affairs.

"Sounds interesting. I think I might try hiking that way today." Laura's headache was easing and she rationalized she could use some fresh air and exercise anyway.

"Oh, well, I don't know. The whole thing's pretty overgrown. No one uses it anymore, 'cept maybe hunters. And the sheriff didn't want you goin' out in the woods," Hattie Perkins reminded.

"I'll probably stick to what's left of the road. Don't worry, Aunt Hattie, I'll take my phone. And I have the sheriff's number." In spite of herself her stomach fluttered.

Laura's aunt started to speak again, but closed her mouth and looked down at her coffee.

Laura got up and took her dishes to the sink, then turned and hugged the older woman from behind. "I'll be careful. I promise," she said as she squeezed her aunt gently. "I'll probably be out a couple hours at least, but I'm used to hiking in the woods. I'm pretty good at finding my way back, too. Don't worry. I'll be fine."

As Laura headed out into the bright mid-morning sunshine, she stopped at the bottom of the porch steps and looked around. She breathed deep, tilted her face to the sun and closed her eyes. A gentle breezed tousled her hair. Maybe it was the mountain air, or last night's 'good cry', but she did feel much better now. Today was a day of possibilities. And she would face them on her own if that's what she had to do.

Laura passed the overgrown lane that led to the Dillon cabin. She chided herself for it, but she walked on the other side of the wooded path and picked up the pace as she went. Birds sang, squirrels skittered among the trees, and a woodpecker knocked nearby. The wind flirted with the leaves overhead, creating dancing patterns of sunlight on the road. Laura stretched her walk out a bit and thumped her hiking stick to the ground every other step in rhythm.

She stopped now and then to take a few pictures. She noted significant scenery markers, like the large rock at the base of a tall narrow tree and the gnarled tree with a triple trunk. Each grew outward at odd angles before turning upwards. It created a natural seat in the middle.

Traces of the double ruts of a road worn in the earth by carts, probably tractors, and later cars were still visible. But the path was overrun with a mix of wild grasses, bright yellow bear's foot, light blue chicory, pale purple lobelia and an overabundance of other plant life. And nature's excess of poison ivy vines and briars had crept across the path with time.

Laura reached the end of Pond Hill Road and stood half hidden behind a large oak tree. She looked up and down the graveled drive. Then she bit her bottom lip, took a deep breath and headed left on Porter's Hollow, the hickory stick balanced in her right hand.

As she approached the creek road, she had the sudden sense she was being watched. Her feet crunched gravel as she did a hard 360. She took in the surroundings quickly, noting the cliff-like rocks that rose from the edge of the road to her left. She caught movement in the woods and turned in time to see a squirrel scamper up a tree.

Laura glanced around again before heading up Porter's Creek Road. She stepped up the pace till she was out of sight of Porter's Hollow. At last she dropped the tip of the walking stick to the ground and returned to a steady tamping rhythm as she continued up the mountain.

All at once the hair on her arms bristled. She stopped and jerked her head around. Her skin tingled as she held her breath. Something rustled in the brush, maybe thirty to fifty feet off to her left. Not a loud sound, but enough to know it was there.

She waited a long moment as the woods became unnaturally still. She stood poised to react, but seconds later, the birds began to twitter again. The forest came to life once more.

Maybe she'd imagined it, the mind had a strange way of freeze-framing a frightening moment. "Shake it off," she whispered.

Laura hiked along Porter's Creek Road about fifteen minutes before she spotted an irregular break in the trees. It cut left up the mountain between two stands of tall pine trees, but the path disappeared into brush only a few feet in. She couldn't see very far ahead. Laura pulled the lightweight pigskin gloves out of her back pocket, and the hunting knife she carried. It wasn't much, but it would have to do.

She tucked her camera into its protective case, pushed it around to hang from her back and started up the mountain. She planned to mark the path with a small can of trail-marking paint she kept in her camera bag. It was the easiest method. She couldn't imagine anybody would mind way out here, but it would fade in time anyway.

Laura looked into the woods around her again. She paused, held her breath briefly and listened. The sense she was being watched continued to grow. But she knew the feeling could simply come from being alone out here.

Briars snagged at her and the thick brush made it difficult to see very far ahead. Laura concentrated on the faint ruts in the ground to stay on the path. It took her several minutes to break through the undergrowth to a more open area, still wooded but no longer thick with briars and vines. She'd cut and cleared some of it as she went, to make the return trip easier.

Now she stood looking up the mountain slope. It appeared to peak within a quarter mile or so. If there was a cabin up there, she should come across it soon. She turned slowly and finally spotted something resembling the shape of a cabin about a hundred yards up to the left.

Laura moved in cautiously. The structure was still mostly intact, though it was overgrown with vines, the forest slowly reclaiming it. She circled it and found the door on the south-facing side where the mountain dropped off sharply about a football field's length away.

The porch sagged on one end, nearly touching the ground, but the steps looked like they'd been rebuilt, newer than the rest of it at least. The instant her foot touched the bottom step, a gust of wind swept up from behind.

It felt like someone had flipped the back of her hair. Laura drew her shoulders up and turned her head to look behind her. She didn't see anything, but the leaves and brush continued to rustle.

She shrugged off the feeling and stepped onto the porch. The cabin door hung crooked and stood open a few inches. Its rusted hinges broke free with a cracking sound as she pushed inward. Dust puffed up from everywhere, creating a cloud of particles that floated on sunbeams, penetrating the woods.

As Laura stood with her hand on the doorknob watching the flecks rise up through the beams, the yellow light of day began to fade. It grew dimmer, and dimmer, until it disappeared and the sky outside went grey. Clouds seemed to gather from nowhere.

She shivered as she stepped into the dark interior. She hadn't thought to bring a flashlight, but she had the app on her mobile phone. Its light illuminated a simple two-room cabin of rough wood, cobwebbed, dusty and barren.

Laura had to force the door further open. It scraped the floor and got stuck at a forty-five-degree angle. She ventured in, checking the kitchen area. The rough sink still had a rusty old metal bucket sitting in it. Its inside was stained a blackened-reddish color.

She opened the tattered curtains that hid the few cupboard shelves. They were bare. Even the furniture, if there had been any, was gone. The fireplace still smelled faintly of ashes but was mostly cleaned out.

The bedroom, however, had a crude rope-bed frame sitting in it. The rotting mattress lay on an angle against the edge of the bed and the floor. Laura noticed the dust under it was smudged—as if it had recently been shoved off the side and had rubbed the floor as it slid to a stop.

When she aimed her phone light at the area, Laura saw a small piece of white paper tacked to the bedpost. She stood still and glanced around the room before reaching for the note. It was smaller than the first one she'd found, but its message was clear. "GO HOM!"

A loud scrape grabbed her attention. *The door!* Someone had shut the cabin door. Laura doused the phone light and backed up to the wall. Floorboards creaked and the house got darker. Her eyes were still adjusting to the change when she heard a loud crash. It sounded like the bucket hit the floor.

Laura slid her body along the wall to try to get a view of the main room. The door was pushed to, but she could see a sliver of dim light at the open edge. She'd have to pull the door hard to get it open enough to get out. But she'd have to cross the room first. Her mind swirled.

There was a window to her left in the bedroom. Most of its panes were already gone or broken. It wasn't far off the ground, and—

Laura froze. A low visceral growl rose from the other room and a large shape with its back to her appeared at the sink. Her dreams of a human-like wolf creature flashed through her mind.

She willed herself to move, taking the three strides to the window as quietly as possible. The open sash was stuck partway— she hoped it was enough. She dropped her camera bag, hiking stick and hoody out the window. She'd have to go head first, *tuck and roll.*

The instant her feet left the floor, something grabbed her shirt from behind. Laura scrambled hard, clutching the window ledge to pull herself through as she felt a searing pain in her back. Whatever had a hold of her was ripping at her shirt and tearing into her skin.

In the next instant, she was pulled back into the room. She whacked her head on the window ledge as she went down, and hit the floor with a thud.

Dizzy and disoriented, she gagged at the sudden stench of animal musk and moldering ash. Before she could get to her feet the thing ripped at her leg and latched onto her ankle. It pulled her further into the darkened room as it turned toward her. She looked into its eyes, mesmerized as they went from yellow-amber to a dark blood-red, just before it raised an arm to slash at her again.

Survival instinct kicked in. Laura jabbed out with the hunting knife she still clutched in one hand. She slammed it into the creature's thigh and groin area several times. The slicing blow the beast had meant to deliver didn't go as deep as it might have, but Laura felt a stinging pain register in her shoulder as she rolled and kicked free of its grip.

It growled deep then and Laura saw a flash of yellow teeth. The creature was about to come at her again when something made it stop and jerk backward. Its eyes cooled to yellow-amber as Laura heard someone grunt.

"Nuh-uh! Nn-nn-nn-nn-noooooo!" the voice commanded.

The creature turned away from her and she glimpsed Loy Porter leading the thing out of the cabin by its shirt front.

A wave of nausea swept over Laura, but she thought the creature looked smaller as it walked away. She stared after the pair a few seconds before she snapped out of her daze and clambered to her feet. She was torn and bleeding. She had to get back to Aunt Hattie's before shock hit and she passed out.

Laura managed to scramble through the window. Pain seared through her shoulder and legs. Outside, she grabbed her things and jumped to her feet. The pain in her back and leg slowed her down. Her shoulder was oozing red, but she moved as fast as she could, heading into the thick brush behind the cabin. She was breathing hard when she stopped to listen.

She had to get her bearings, quickly. Noting the direction she'd come, she began a slow circle the other way to get back to the trail. She stayed wide of the cabin and crept low. Wincing at the stinging pain that invaded her body, she tried to make as little noise as possible. She hoped to get to the trail before that thing had time to change its mind and come after her again.

The air went still and the woods fell silent. She imagined him out there somewhere nearby listening for her. Then she heard a familiar crashing in the woods. The creature didn't seem to care how much racket it made. *Why should it?*

Laura used the noise to cover her own, and reached the opening to the trail as she heard it snarl again nearby. It was somewhere on the other side of the cabin as she limped down the mountain.

CHAPTER 28

LOY

Wednesday, October 13, 2010

Loy's body was shaking bad and his pants were wet.

He'd never faced the beast himself before.

But Curry was still his brother. He'd followed him early in the morning to keep an eye on him like Glen told him to.

Loy knew where he was going. Curry was headed out to the caves and he'd be gone all day.

The beast must've got wind of Miss Laura's scent on the air while Loy was napping in the woods.

He woke to the growling sound. He hadn't meant to step in, but he couldn't stand by and let it hurt her.

Loy stopped the thing, and Curry started to come back to himself. But then he heard her stomping around back in the brush and went after her again.

Loy followed, not sure what to do. But she must've outsmarted the beast 'cause he found Curry sitting on the cabin porch with his head in his hands, groaning.

Loy hid in the trees not far off till Curry shook his head, stood up tall and stretched his neck, and walked off down the mountain.

CHAPTER 29

LAURA

Wednesday, October 13, 2010

When Laura left the Hadley cabin, she managed to work her way back through the brush to where the lane opened up onto Porter's Creek Road. Someone grabbed her as she stumbled out of the trees. Her head felt light and her vision blurred. She fought against his grip.

"Whoa, hey, what's going on?" Her brother held her upper arms to keep her from going down. What happened to you?" he exclaimed as he got a good look at her condition.

"Run," Laura struggled to speak. "We have to run," she managed before she passed out.

Laura came to as Tom eased her into the passenger seat of his truck. He looked her over briefly, then got behind the wheel. "You're going straight to the hospital," he declared. As he started the engine he shook his head. "I knew you'd do this. I just knew you'd have to come out here on your own," he declared.

At the hospital, they admitted Laura overnight as soon as they cleaned, mended and bandaged her wounds. They also decided to give her an IV antibiotic since she appeared to have been attacked by an animal.

Tom stood by her now, gripping the bedrail, knuckles white. "You going tell me what happened out there?" he asked.

"I'm not ready for the sheriff to know everything—not yet anyway. He'd probably take over and keep me out of the search if he knew."

Tom pressed his lips together and sighed, but nodded his agreement. She pulled out the note she'd found and handed it to him.

"There, that's proof if you don't believe me. Somebody followed me into that cabin. He must have gotten ahead of me somehow and put that on the bedpost. Or else he knew I was coming and set me up ahead of time."

Laura grimaced as she handed the note to Tom, stretching the skin along the stitches she'd needed across her shoulder. Her brother didn't look as skeptical as she thought he would as he read the scrap of paper. He tilted his head and looked at her.

"Whatever grabbed me," she continued, "it wasn't human. But it wasn't entirely animal either. I can't explain it, but somehow I get the sense that Curry Porter is behind it all. Loy stopped that thing somehow . . . he saved my life."

"These notes," Tom waved the paper in the air, "they don't really threaten you. They're just telling you to go home. Whoever wrote them doesn't want you here, but this person doesn't mean to hurt you if you don't go. As far as the attack, you probably surprised a black bear in there scavenging for food."

Laura couldn't believe her ears! *Were all brothers like this?* Did he not listen to anything she'd told him?

Tom shook his head and gave a frustrated sigh. "You know, maybe if you just stopped snooping around looking for Glen, whoever this is would leave you alone to have a nice visit with your Aunt Hattie."

Laura stared at him, mouth open, eyes wide. *Are you serious?* "How can I just walk away and forget him when . . . he's reaching out—to me. I can't just give up now. No way," she declared.

Tom's shoulders lifted as he sighed deep. He looked down at his own hands and set his mouth in a tight line. Then he shrugged his shoulders. "It was Curry that came and got me the night Glen got attacked. He came to get *my* help, and I was only thirteen."

Laura looked up quickly, studying his face.

Tom paused as if thinking, "You know, Loy might be the retarded one, pardon the term, but there was always something strange about Curry, too. Just in a different way. He's not really—normal—to say the least. He'll defend family to the last but he's hard-edged and gruff. Even the people he loves, he loves grudgingly. If it hadn't been for my daddy, I'd have avoided him completely," Tom declared.

He shook his head and let out a deep breath. Laura waited silently, hoping he'd continue.

"Curry may still be hiding our father, but I doubt it'd be against his own will. It wasn't back then." He shook his head again, "The only thing holding Glen captive back then was his own fears."

"But if he isn't being held against his will," Laura objected, "then how do you explain the phone calls?"

Tom thought for a moment and replied, "My guess is he might be sick, not clear-minded. Maybe the beginnings of Alzheimer's. I don't know."

"But he remembers me by name, and he hasn't seen me in forty years. That's not Alzheimer's," Laura couldn't contain her frustration.

Tom scrunched his face in thought, "Maybe not. But age-onset dementia can do that. People remember things from when they were children, but can't remember who visited them yesterday. They get disoriented, connect things that don't go together."

"But he sounded so clear," Laura argued. "I work with people every day who have problems like that. I'd know."

"Listen, Laura, if I can't deter you from keeping up this search, would you do one thing for me at least? Would you wait till I have the chance to go see Curry myself and have a talk with him? If our father's still alive and he knows where he is, maybe I can reason with him if I can get him face to face."

"You've suspected it was him all along, haven't you?" she accused.

"What I might suspect, and what I can say for sure are miles apart. But I'm still not positive," Tom shrugged. "He's avoided me since I came back. I've stopped in at Beulah's a few times, and I've seen his truck around. But he's never shown his face while I was there."

The preacher looked away, then he raised his eyes to her face and went on, "But I'll see what I can do to find him."

"If you're going to talk to him, I want to come with you," Laura insisted.

"Not a good idea. Especially if he's already feeling hostile about you being here. Besides, you need to rest up and recover. Let me talk to him. I'll let you know what I find out. And then, if necessary, we'll go to Sheriff Wilson about it."

Laura recognized the look of determination on Tom's face. He wouldn't take her along. She'd have to find another way to confront Curry Porter.

"All right, fine. But when can you go?" Laura would wait, but not long.

"Well, we've got prayer meeting tonight and a church board meeting tomorrow. They can both run pretty long and late. I'll see what I can do on Saturday."

Two days? Laura didn't have the patience for that. But when she spoke, she tried to keep the frustration out of her voice. "Okay. Then you'll call me afterward. Right away?" she pressed.

Aunt Hattie entered the hospital room at that moment. She smiled reassuringly and patted Laura's arm. "Goodness, young lady, what happened to you?"

Tom spoke up, "I believe she got jumped by an angry black bear."

"Oh, your momma will be fit to be tied if she sees you like this."

"What?" Laura's eyes widened, "Momma? What do you mean?"

"Yes, she called. Asked how you were doin', chatted a bit. Said she'd be here sometime tomorrow. Wanted to know if that was okay. Imagine that! Asking the only Momma you ever knew if it's okay if you visit. People sure are different up north, ain't they?"

Laura's mouth dropped open as she stared at Hattie Perkins. Robey was coming here. Now. Just when she was so close to finding her father. And now that she knew about her only brother, she wasn't looking forward to a confrontation.

What on earth could have moved Roberta Maitlin to return to the "hillbilly hell" she'd struggled so hard to leave behind?

CHAPTER 30

CURRY

Wednesday, October 13, 2010

The caves on the other side of the mountain from Porter's Hollow had low ceilings. So low a grown man had to stoop to walk around. At least one as tall as Curry Porter. But they were his real lair, his hideaway.

They were cool and dark. He found comfort and solace there. Especially after the beast left him. His blood boiled and his head felt near to bursting afterward. And there was a bitter taste of sulphur in his mouth.

But the bad taste left behind this time was more because he'd let that woman slip away. Loy wasn't supposed to be there. He'd told him before to stay away when the beast was around. He didn't want to hurt his brothers, but he couldn't help them if they chose not to listen.

Curry seethed. That upstart daughter of Glen's from Pennsylvania was traipsing around his hollow, his woods, like she had a right to be there.

But he'd show her soon enough. No woman would ever get the better of him.

CHAPTER 31

LAURA

Thursday, October 14, 2010

It was just about supper time when Roberta Maitlin finally pulled up in front of Aunt Hattie's. Laura hadn't been able to sit still for the past two hours. She'd checked out front every ten minutes.

At last she'd gone into the kitchen and busied herself with dinner preparations. She set the table, peeled potatoes, washed the pots, and rearranged the table several times until Aunt Hattie had told her to go sit down and rest.

"You're still gimpin' on that leg a bit, and I think you've got a spot of blood on the back of your shirt. Might want to change 'fore your momma sees you. Freshen up and go set a spell," the older woman insisted.

Laura changed and tried to relax, but she still found herself jumping up to check outside at every sound. Yet, when she finally heard the car tires crunch in the gravel, she hesitated. Her mind raced ahead again to what she could say to convince her mother not to interfere with her efforts to find Glen Porter. But the knock on the door came too soon.

Laura jumped up and glanced toward the kitchen as she went. Where was Aunt Hattie? Hadn't she heard the car? Laura caught a glimpse of her dress as the older woman rounded the corner into the pantry out of sight. Appeared she was making herself scarce intentionally. *Ah, well. Probably for the best.*

"Laura, could you give me a hand with these bags, dear?" Robey rushed in to fill the moment.

Awkward hellos, and even more so, awkward goodbyes were ungraceful. *"Stand up straight, speak first. Makes a good impression. It gives you control of the moment,"* her mother would say.

Laura gingerly took one of her mother's bags and set it down near the stairs. She turned to ask how the drive had been, but Robey had begun to wander around the room. She picked up pictures and knickknacks, studying them.

Emotions seemed to chase themselves across her face. Laura thought she even saw a faint smile when Robey picked up a photo of herself with Laura as a toddler holding a kitten.

She set the picture frame down again and her expression returned to normal. "So how have you been?" Robey asked in her polite formal way.

Laura thought a moment before she answered. She didn't want to bring on a confrontation now. "I've been enjoying the mountain air. I'd forgotten how beautiful it is down here," she ventured.

"I suppose it is, in a rugged sort of way. A bit too rugged for my taste anymore." Robey seemed to hesitate. "Where's Aunt Hattie?"

"She's in the kitchen. I think supper is almost ready," Laura answered just as Hattie Perkins entered the room.

The older woman went straight to Robey and wrapped her in a big hug. "My lands, it's good to see you. It's been too long," she declared.

To Laura's surprise, her mother returned the hug without reservation. And she swore Robey's eyes glistened. "Yes, well," her mother seemed at a loss for words, "you know how it is. Life gets so busy and you lose track of time. And before you know it, years have slipped by." Robey stepped back. "How are you, Aunt Hattie?" She looked the older woman over briefly. "You look like you're doing well."

"Oh well, the arthritis kicks up sometimes, but I cain't really complain. Doin' all right for an old hillbilly woman, I s'pose. I was real sorry to hear 'bout your husband passin'."

"Thank you, it's an adjustment, but you get through it. You've been there yourself, and you were much younger. You've done well keeping things together all these years," Robey said as she rubbed Hattie's shoulder and back.

Was that empathy she heard in her mother's voice? Somehow the setting seemed to change her. It was subtle, but this was a side of her Laura was unfamiliar with. Could just being back here again have thawed something in Robey's heart?

"Well, now, are you two ready to sit down to supper? Ain't nothin' fancy, just ham and green beans and potatoes, and some black-eyed peas with cornbread. Hope you're hungry." Aunt Hattie bustled them into the kitchen. The food was already on the table.

The three of them took the places they'd used years ago, almost instinctively, as if time had stood still. Habit made a comfortable niche to return to. It turned time itself into an old friend, allowing them to pick up where they'd left off with ease.

As they made small talk over dinner, Robey asked about the scratches peeking out from the edge of Laura's t-shirt.

"It's nothing," Laura quickly replied. "I was out hiking and got into some briars. Had trouble getting through them."

Aunt Hattie made no reply.

When supper was cleared, Laura helped Robey get her things up to her old room. Robey sat down on the bed and tucked her hands together on her lap. She looked around the room and sighed. Laura stopped by the door, unsure whether to say goodnight and make a polite exit, or to ask her mother if she was okay.

Robey looked up at her then, holding Laura's gaze a long moment. "Come sit down a minute." She patted the bed as she spoke.

Laura obeyed like a child. She glanced at her mother, then looked down at her own clasped hands.

But Robey was silent so long, Laura decided to speak. "Why did you come here, Mom? You know, for years I was angry at you—at first, because I thought it was all your fault. You took us away. But later, I was angry at *him* because he disappeared on us. I wanted to stop needing to be daddy's little girl and grow up."

Robey sat motionless. Laura couldn't read her expression. She decided to keep going. "Why didn't you tell me I had a brother? Did my father go into hiding because of me? Was it something to do with me finding Lottie Edwards' body?"

Robey looked away, her shoulders drooped. "I never wanted you to be hurt. Not like I was—ever. I wanted your life to be safe, happy, uncomplicated. A child should never have to bear the weight of her mother's pain, and especially not her father's guilt."

Laura watched her mother's face. Her brow furrowed, her eyes reflecting the pain from years of buried grief. How had she managed to hide this side of her all this time?

"But it was never your fault, Laura. What your father and his brothers did—what I believe they were responsible for—should never have been allowed to go unpunished. I was so angry, and so—sorry you had to be the one to find that child." After a brief pause she went on, "You were way too young to understand at the time. And when you did ask questions, I just didn't know how to explain it so you could."

Robey closed her eyes and rubbed her forehead.

"Then it just got easier not to talk about it. You had a father, in your stepdad Howard. He took good care of you financially and physically. You—we—had a safe, normal, easy life. I didn't want to spoil that. I didn't want you to spoil it."

Laura watched Robey's face as she spoke. Her eyes glistened, her brow creased. "I found out Glen was alive from Curry. He told me he was hiding out from the thing that attacked them. I managed to get him to take me to see your father the day before we left." Robey squeezed the tears from her eyes and sighed. "I tried to get Glen to talk about what happened, to face the truth and go to the police if that's what it meant. But he refused. He said he couldn't because 'the beast' would kill him if he did."

Robey was pale now. Her hands were shaking as she spoke.

"So, I tried to get him to leave with us. He said his guilt and shame would only poison what we had, that I should take you and go. And stay away forever. Even gave me a few hundred dollars he'd saved up. I took it and bought that junky car we had.

"The next morning, I went back one more time to give him another chance to change his mind. When I went in he was sitting in an old rocker, head down, brooding." Robey shuddered and wrapped her arms around herself.

Laura put an arm around her mother then, but waited quietly till Robey went on.

"He didn't even look up at first when I spoke. Then all of a sudden, out of the blue, he jumped up, threw the chair back and came at me. He got me by both shoulders and pinned my back to the wall. Then he got right up in my face and practically growled, *'Get out! Go away and never come back—and take the girl with you. Now!'* "

A deep sigh escaped her. Laura gave her mother's shoulder a gentle squeeze.

"I ran out the door then, but Curry was there on the porch. He must have been listening. He grabbed me by the waist, picked me up off the floor and held me close to his face. His eyes seemed to turn darker and his voice sounded—evil. He growled at me to do what I was told, if I cared about you at all.

"So I did. That was the morning we left North Carolina for good. At least I thought it was. I ran then because I was afraid. And I never came back—until now. And only because you wanted to. And that makes me afraid for you." Robey's unshed tears began to fall at last.

Her whole body sagged further into the mattress. Laura had never seen her like this. She pulled her close, and laid her head against her mother's, drawing comfort from the touch.

When Laura went to bed later, she tossed and turned till she fell into a fitful slumber. The shadow-wolf returned to her dreams again, only this time he had a face—a human face—and he wore a hooded cloak. But no matter how hard she tried to see who it was, she couldn't.

At first, she was a bystander, watching the creature from the side as it bent over something. She drew as near as she dared and what she saw made her tremble. A small blue mound on the earth beneath him turned into the frightened little girl with blonde hair and slanted eyes.

Her mouth was open in a silent scream and she thrashed wildly under his heavy claw hands. Laura's horror grew as she watched because she sensed what the evil creature was about to do—and it was vile.

Then, suddenly, she became the little girl again. Pain seared her body like a hot branding iron. She woke herself with a strangled cry, barely managing to hold back her own screams.

Laura stumbled to the bathroom and gagged over the toilet. She struggled to catch her breath as she dropped to the floor. "It was a dream," she told herself. "It was just a dream."

But it was so real. She still felt suffocated and violated all at once. She hated those kinds of dreams, the ones that made you wake confused—sure what you saw really happened.

She'd never had one quite like this though. This dream had been so real she still felt the weight of the creature's body, the uncomfortable burning sensation below; and the air in the room was foul with its scent.

Laura wrapped the bathrobe tighter around herself and stood. The room spun, but she steadied herself with a hand on the sink. She splashed cool water on her face then and looked at the clock. It was 4:30 a.m., no use trying to go back to bed. She walked softly down the stairs to the kitchen and made a cup of hot tea with sugar and thick, sweet, real cream. Fattening but comforting.

Laura sat on the sofa, legs curled up under her, and turned the TV on. She found a channel with a talk show, sipped her tea and focused on the screen, determined not to replay the dream in her mind again.

Finally, she set the empty cup down and let the drone of the television put her in a captive trance. Somewhere in the wee hours of the morning she drifted into a peaceful, dreamless sleep at last.

CHAPTER 32

LOY

Thursday, October 14, 2010

Miss Laura was in danger.

Curry was mad at him 'cause he'd interfered. But he couldn't let her get dead.

Glen would kill him if that happened.

But Miss Laura got away. She made it out of the woods and Tom was there to help her.

And now Glen wanted him to go check on her. Told him to watch and listen a while. Then come back and tell him things.

Loy was hidden in the tree line when they pulled in. Miss Laura walked kind of stiff, but she looked okay.

He sat a while but it got so quiet, he fell asleep.

He sat right up, though, when he heard another car.

The woman who got out was old now, but he knew her right away.

Loy ran back to the shed at home. He pushed the four-wheeler out the back. Then he started it up and headed through the woods to Curry's house.

Glen was inside eating dinner when he got there.

He pert near choked when Loy scratched out the words he couldn't say. "ROBY HEER!"

Glen grabbed the paper and stared at it. "Robey?" he asked. "My Robey?"

Loy nodded hard.

Glen stood up then, "You still got that note I gave you for Laurie?"

Loy pulled it out of his back pocket. Glen grabbed it and wrote some more stuff in his shaky handwriting.

"You get this to her somehow. Soon." He grabbed Loy by both arms then and got up in his face. "They got to—stay—away—from Curry. You got to get this to my Laurie, you hear me?"

Loy nodded his head, eyes wide. He understood.

CHAPTER 33

LAURA

Friday morning, October 15, 2010

The morning after Laura's mother came to Grassy Creek, Sheriff Wilson decided to pay a call. But Laura didn't wake up till she heard the knock at the door. She struggled to remember why she was on the couch in the living room.

The smells from the kitchen made her stomach rumble. And the man's voice in the other room muddled her brain.

Uggh! She had to get upstairs quick. She couldn't let him see her this way.

Laura snuck toward the stairway just as she heard Aunt Hattie announce, "Oh, she's in the sittin' room. Must a had trouble sleepin' 'cause we found her in there on the sofa with the TV still on when we come down this mornin'. You go on in and tell her breakfast's ready. Then you come join us, too."

Laura dashed for the stairs, but too late.

"Good morning, sleepy head. How are you feeling?" Blaine Wilson caught her trying to tame her morning hair. "Sorry to catch you off guard," he said with grin.

Laura blushed and pulled the robe closed before she stammered, "Good morning. Umm, give me a few minutes to wash up. I'll be right back down." She turned up the steps before he could say anything else.

She ran a wet cloth over her face and changed into jeans and a t-shirt. She had to use some water to tame her hair. As an afterthought, she put on a little foundation and was in the kitchen fifteen minutes later, feeling reasonably human again though her head and body ached.

As the four of them sat down to a hearty breakfast, Laura couldn't help thinking how strange the situation felt. She and her mother back here together as adults, with an aging Hattie Perkins, while the local sheriff joined them for a meal like, well, like family.

When they finished breakfast, Aunt Hattie shooed Laura and Blaine out of the kitchen while she and Robey stayed to clean up. He shook his head with a laugh. But the sheriff's expression turned serious as they stepped out onto the porch in the morning sunlight.

He turned toward her, studying her face, "Should've known the preacher was related to you," he said. "You can see it in the face."

"What? Who told you?" Laura found herself disconcerted again.

"He did. Called me last evening. Said you were out investigating the woods again. Ended up in the hospital overnight, I hear. Tom suggested maybe I should lock you up to keep you safe," he appeared to be only half-joking. "The reverend said you were attacked by something. Maybe a black bear. He also thought you might have run across Curry Porter out there. Something about finding another note, and being chased."

Blaine Wilson continued to watch her face, but he stood quietly. Laura shoved her hands into her pants pockets and looked down. He probably wouldn't believe her if she told him what really happened. She shook her head and shrugged.

"It wasn't a black bear that grabbed me. I was up at the old Hadley cabin above Porter's Creek Road. I found a note inside on the bedpost before I was attacked."

The sheriff pulled out his notebook, flipped it open and clicked his pen. He was all business again. "That's what the reverend said. Can I see the note?"

Laura handed it to him. He pulled the other one from his shirt pocket to compare them. "Sure looks like the same printing. So can you describe what you think attacked you?"

Laura hesitated. "It was dark in the cabin. I was back in the bedroom. Then the cabin door scraped shut and I realized I wasn't alone. I hid back out of sight and was able to see the shape of someone in what looked like a hooded jacket and dark clothes. It had to be a man. I decided to try to sneak out the window while he was rattling around making noise. But, like I said, he grabbed at my leg and started—mauling—me."

She stopped and looked up at him before she continued.

"I had a pocket knife so I fought back. I drew blood, but he couldn't have been hurt very badly. I must have startled the . . ." Laura paused trying to decide what to call the thing that attacked her, ". . . creature, person, or whatever it was, because he lost his grip. I managed to get out of the cabin and run into the woods behind it. I guess I lost him long enough to get my bearings. Then I circled back to the trail. I made it back out to Porter's Creek Road, and that's where I ran into Tom."

Laura didn't tell Blaine Wilson about Loy and the way the thing had followed him.

The sheriff had been busy making notes as she talked. When he looked up, his eyebrows were drawn into a contemplative crease. "What made you want to check out the old Hadley place, anyway?"

Laura hesitated. She wondered just how much her brother had told him, and why he'd changed his mind about talking to the sheriff at all.

"I remembered hearing stories about it when I was a little girl, so I asked Aunt Hattie about it. I just wanted to get out for a good hike, and I thought it would be an interesting site to take pictures."

Laura decided a half-truth wasn't an outright lie at least. She really had heard stories when she was young. She just didn't think she should be the one to reveal Tom's secrets about the place.

The sheriff jotted something in his notepad and tucked it away. "You won't mind me keeping this other note too, will you?"

Laura shook her head and shrugged, "I don't need them."

Blaine Wilson put one foot on the porch steps and one hand on his knee. Hat tucked under his arm, he leaned in toward the porch where she stood above him.

After a moment, he tilted his head and looked up at her. "I've got to say, you're worrying me some, Miss Laura. Pennsylvania city girl alone in these woods. You could get lost and nobody'd find you for days. And with these notes, and the phone calls, I'm not sure what exactly is going on. But somebody is trying to scare you off at least. And at worst? You could get seriously hurt." The look on his face seemed to indicate he thought that would be terrible.

Laura felt a nervous flutter in her gut. Still she couldn't help getting her feathers ruffled when he suggested she shouldn't walk alone in the woods.

"I can take care of myself on the trail well enough, Sheriff. And I'm not sure what, or who attacked me. But yes, I agree. Someone obviously doesn't want me here. I can't let that stop me now, though." She watched his expression grow even more solemn.

He seemed to mull things over as he set his foot on the ground and ran the fingers of his left hand back and forth along the brim of his hat. He kept his gaze fixed.

"I went out to Beulah Porter's. Couldn't find Curry. His truck was there, but I'm guessing he saw me pull in and high-tailed it. Tried to get Loy to take me to him. His eyes got real big, and he shook his head hard like he was afraid. Then he ran off to the shed and shut himself in with that old hound of his."

He looked up at Laura then.

"I don't know Loy that well. Used to see him walking around Jefferson sometimes, but not for a while now. He liked the library. He'd go there to read, even learned to use the computers according to Mrs. Blakely, the librarian. She says he's a bit smarter than most folks think."

Laura looked at the sheriff. *Where was he going with this?*

"You know how sometimes when you're looking for something, you can miss the forest for the trees?" He glanced up at her again. "I'm just thinking out loud, but you might need to be more careful than you think. Those two are brothers, and blood is still thicker than water down here. You'd do well to keep that in mind."

Laura sighed and shifted her weight to her left foot.

The sheriff straightened and put his hat on. "I've got a few other matters to attend to this afternoon, but I told Beulah I'd need to see Curry. I'll try again tomorrow morning. Meanwhile I'm going to have to insist you stay out of the woods till I figure out who's behind all this. Wouldn't want the pretty Pennsylvania lady to get hurt visiting our fair state now, would we?" He gave a wry grin, but Laura got the impression he meant what he said.

Blaine Wilson nodded his head and tipped his hat as he slid his lithe frame into the SUV.

As Laura opened the screen door, her mother stepped back. Robey looked at her, eyebrows raised, a smile twitching at the corners of her mouth.

Laura huffed out a sigh and shook her head, "It's not like that."

Robey's eyebrows rose higher.

"For goodness sake. I wouldn't be ready for . . ." Laura stopped and shook her head again, then made a quick escape up the stairs to shower.

When Laura came back down a little while later, her mother was gone. For some reason it disconcerted her. Aunt Hattie said Robey wanted to do some shopping and needed to get it done early. She didn't want to be out on the roads after dark since she wasn't as familiar with the area as she used to be.

Strange how she'd want to go off happily shopping alone here when she'd never wanted to come back at all. It occurred to Laura her mother might prefer to reacquaint herself with things on her own so her daughter wouldn't witness any lingering vulnerability. But she'd been so genuine the night before, completely open.

Or was she?

Laura wondered if there was still more Robey wasn't telling her. She sighed. *Secrets again—always more secrets.*

CHAPTER 34

LAURA

Friday, early afternoon, October 15, 2010

Tom had promised to find Curry and talk to him on Saturday evening. The sheriff had said he would try again in the morning. Neither one knew of the other one's plans, and neither one planned to see the man today.

Aunt Hattie had gone to lay down to ease her aching joints, and her mother had gone off earlier without saying exactly where. All the while Laura sat on a rocker on the front porch with a cup of tea as she tried to determine what her next step should be. She felt edgy. She couldn't just sit around and wait for someone else to take care of things. She'd had enough of that.

She wondered if she could find Curry Porter's trailer on her own. There had to be a way. Maybe Beulah would tell her more. But what if Curry or Loy were there?

The late morning sun glistened on the stones in the driveway. Laura watched as birds skittered through the trees and a squirrel darted across the path. The sound of a gentle breeze whispered through the leaves. Too bad such a beautiful, peaceful setting had to be marred by dark thoughts and dreams. She shivered.

Laura decided she'd have to take the risk. And now was the time, with Robey gone and Hattie asleep upstairs.

She slipped into the house and grabbed her purse and car keys. Then she scribbled a quick note to Aunt Hattie, *'Went for a drive. Visiting Grannie Beulah. Be back in a couple hours or so. Love you.'* She signed it, *'Laura Allen.'*

Curry Porter's truck was nowhere in sight when she pulled up at her grandmother's house. She listened for the hound as she stepped out of the Jeep, but all was quiet. Maybe this would be easier than she thought.

She knocked loud and hard until she heard a familiar shuffle at the door. Then she called out, "Beulah, it's Laura Allen." The door opened a few inches and the elderly woman appeared. "Good morning, how are you today?" Laura asked.

"Fair to middlin'." Beulah Porter put a hand to her own back. "Fair to middlin'," she repeated after taking stock of her own condition. "You come on in, then. I cain't get this bean soup open I was plannin' on for lunch." She held a can out into the air for Laura who took it on cue and followed the elderly woman to the kitchen.

Laura fixed the soup for Beulah and helped her make a sandwich. She forced herself to relax and enjoy small talk with the older woman. Beulah was slow to open up, and she didn't want to make her suspicious.

Laura cleaned up the few dishes she'd used and watched in amazement as Beulah dried them and put each one carefully in place from memory.

Then without a word Beulah got up and proceeded to get cups out and put water on for tea. She put the cups on the table and sat in silence. When the kettle whistled, she got up and got it herself, even poured the hot water. When the older woman sat down to her tea, Laura finally spoke.

"I didn't see Loy or Curry about when I pulled in. You by yourself today?" she asked to guide the direction of the conversation.

"Well, now, Loy's probl'y off in the woods with that hound a his. I 'spect Curry'll be around 'fore too long. Takes care a his momma, that boy does. And his brothers. But I do all right on my own most a the time, long as they check in on me now and then." Beulah spoke slow and deliberate with a hint of belligerent pride in her voice.

"You do very well. But it's good they watch out for you." Laura's concern was sincere. "You told me Curry has a trailer over in Lansing, didn't you?"

Beulah nodded her head, "He does. An' it's a good sized one. Got two bedrooms and two bathrooms. It's right comfortable. Heated too an' it's got a shed out back."

"Oh, have you been there?" Laura asked.

"Been out there a few times. When I could still see a might. Don't go out much a nowhere no more. Not since the glaucoma."

"Did he ever marry or have children?" Laura pressed on.

"Naw. Cur ain't ever took that kind a likin' to any one woman. Had girlfriends a plenty, but he just never had a marryin' feelin' toward any of 'em, I guess. He lives down there on his own. Loy stays with him now and then. I got a picture of the place somewhere in the hutch." Beulah got up and led Laura over to a large antique wooden cupboard with glass doors on the top half.

She pulled a stack of photo albums out of the bottom side door. There were several vinyl-covered books filled with mostly older black and white pictures.

"It's in the red one, I think. That's the newer stuff." Beulah handed them to her.

They sat back down at the table. Laura leafed through the pages, read the notes and dates, struck by the history contained there. Long-ago moments captured forever—a family's legacy in black and white, and Kodachrome.

There were photos of her father with people she'd never seen. The notes beneath indicated his wife, his father, other family names. Aunt Beulah told her the stories behind many of them as she paged along. At last she came to a color photo of a tan and white trailer, with Curry Porter standing on the wooden steps in front of it.

"Yep, that's it then," the other woman assured as Laura described it.

"Hmm, looks like it's out in the country, not right in Lansing?"

Beulah nodded, "My boy, Cur, don't much like people around close. I visited there a few times, so I 'member it well. I got a picture in my head. Cain't see them in the books no more. But I got most of 'em right up here," she said as she tapped her temple.

"It looks like there's a road sign over to the right of the picture. But I can't read it," Laura commented as she studied the photo.

"That'd be Buck Tail Lane. It's the only place back there. It's why Curry bought it. 'Tain't far off the main road toward Big Horse Creek, but it ain't too close to others neither. 'Bout twenty-five minutes from here I'd say, off a 194 headin' into Lansing." Beulah Porter seemed pleased to be able to recall and describe things so well. Things she could only see in her mind's eye.

Laura visited with the elderly woman for more than an hour. She enjoyed listening to her stories, and Beulah lost the edge in her voice when she talked about her family.

But Laura began to feel an urgency to get on the road before it got late. She didn't want dark to descend before she had a chance to find Buck Tail Lane. And she didn't want to still be at Beulah Porter's when Curry or Loy came back. She eased into her goodbyes as soon as possible without being rude. Then she headed out the drive quickly, hoping she hadn't been spotted by anyone.

When she was back on Old Route 16, she pulled over to look up directions to Lansing on the GPS. It was still early afternoon, and it didn't look too complicated. She ought to be able to find her way, but she started to wonder if she should tell someone where she was headed.

This might be her opportunity to find out where her father was at last. She couldn't think of anyone who wouldn't try to stop her if they knew, though. Except maybe her daughter, Tara.

"Hey, Mom. How's it going?" Tara answered on the second ring. "Thought you were never going to call. How are you? I was starting to worry."

"I'm fine. But things have gotten a little—complicated—and weird. Your grandma decided to show up here yesterday. And now she's out *shopping.*" Laura couldn't keep the frustration out of her voice.

"Really? Whatever possessed her to do that?" Tara laughed.

"I'm not sure exactly, but we talked a lot last night. It was the first time in a long time we really connected, or at least I think we did," Laura paused. "Listen Tara, there's a lot I need to tell you about, but right now I'm on my way to visit my Uncle Curry's place. He knows more than he's been saying about my father and I'm hoping to figure this out and get things settled soon. I can't go into it all right now. Just wanted to touch base, say hello and let you know what's going on."

"Well, I'm just glad you called finally," Tara half-scolded her.

"Did you start your new job yet—no, wait, that's next week, isn't it?" Laura had been so preoccupied she'd forgotten what day it was.

"Mmm hmm, next Monday. But I'm going in tomorrow to spend some time getting familiar with the place, meet my class, and spend the afternoon helping the teacher that's leaving."

"Oh? That's nice. You'll get some time with the children before you just walk in and take over. Sounds good." Laura was excited for Tara.

"Yup. I'm kind of nervous, but I'm looking forward to it. Anyway, are you sure you should confront your uncle on your own? It kind of sounds like he might not be too friendly. From your description of him, I mean."

Was Tara starting to doubt her too?

"Well, I'm not going to wait around for everyone else to decide what I should or shouldn't do about it. I get the feeling everyone wants to put me off." Laura felt herself getting snippy. "I'm pretty sure there are things my mother hasn't told me and maybe doesn't want me to ever know. Maybe she thought she could stop me if she came in person. But she disappeared on her own this morning and I haven't seen her since."

"That's odd," Tara mused aloud. "But if anyone would know whether it was safe to be out there searching for your father on your own, she would. Don't you think?"

"I don't know. I think she's protecting herself, her own past. Putting her fears on me," Laura argued.

"Hmm, maybe. Are you still having those dreams you told me about?" Tara asked.

"Yes. The last time the creature had a face, but I couldn't see it. This might sound crazy, but I've been thinking maybe Lottie Edwards is trying to tell me something. Her picture was in the information her father gave me. It was her as a little girl. I saw her clearly in my dreams long before I saw the picture." Laura didn't tell Tara what she thought happened to the girl in her dreams or how she'd felt the assault herself.

"There are people who can solve crimes through paranormal connections like dreams, premonitions, ESP, visions, that kind of stuff. Just never thought you'd be one of them," her daughter joked.

"Well, whatever it is," Laura said, "I've got to see this through. I'll call you tomorrow or maybe Saturday. I need to get going now before it gets dark on me. So, I'll talk to you later. Love you."

"Okay. Love you too. Good luck. And Mom," Tara paused, then added, "be careful."

"I will, bye." Laura tucked the cell phone into her pocket and got back on the road. She sighed and shook her head as drove. Now Tara wanted to discourage her from her search, too.

CHAPTER 35

ROBEY

Friday morning, October 15, 2010

Robey needed to see Reverend Honeywell.

Tom had been with Glen after he disappeared. She'd often wondered what had become of him. She worried he might take his own life.

Well, she'd worried at first. She'd tried to write to him through Curry, but never heard anything back. She even included her phone number at the time and asked him to call.

She'd held out hope for a long time that he would miss them and want to come to Pennsylvania.

Robey stopped at the 7-Eleven to fill her car up. When she got back in the driver's seat her cell phone was ringing. It was her granddaughter, Tara.

"Hello?" Robey answered warmly. She and Tara had always been close, it was easy with her bright personality. Tara was a teacher now, living in Ohio on her own, but she called Grandma often if only to say hello.

Of course, Doug and Laura had a child before Tara. Another little girl. But Robey had been overcome with sorrow, and something akin to panic, when she'd learned Barbara Allen was born—different—the way Lottie Edwards had been different. And then the child died just months after Tara was born. Robey hadn't been able to respond normally to the whole situation. She never even sent a sympathy card or went to the funeral.

With Tara, it was like she'd been given another chance. And she liked to think she'd done a good job loving her, being there for her.

"Hey, Grandma, how are you doing?" Tara interrupted her weary contemplation.

"I'm fine honey, but I'm worried about your mother." Robey didn't want to waste precious time. She had to find a way to help her daughter before she got herself hurt.

"I know. I just talked to her. I'm worried, too. She said she's going to find her Uncle Curry's place and confront him about her father. I thought maybe you should know where she's headed. It sounds a little creepy."

Robey assured Tara she would look out for Laura, and she'd get some help doing it. All the more reason to enlist Tom Honeywell.

Robey pulled up at the preacher's house, her mind far away. She turned off the engine and stayed sitting until Tom knocked on the window. Robey gave a startled gasp and put a hand over her chest as he opened the door for her.

"Oh, you scared the life out of me," she declared.

"Well, bless my soul, if it ain't Robey Foster."

Robey took his offered hand as she got out of the car. "Good to see you again, Tom," she smiled politely. He was taller than Glen, but he had his father's eyes and features. A handsome man. Her heart squeezed with pain at the memories she hadn't thought of in years. Not until she went through the old pictures, preparing to come down here and . . . what?

Try to talk Laura out of her quest? She'd thought so at first. But when she'd seen her there in Aunt Hattie's living room, the years melted away. In her mind she saw the bubbly little girl her daughter had been back before all this. Full of laughter, love, hope and insatiable curiosity. She'd had such a bold, lively personality when she was little. Where had that Laura been all these years?

Robey had seen the spark in her eyes again when she'd arrived. Maybe her daughter did need to reconnect with her father. But Robey wasn't sure the truth of what happened back then was something either of them would want to deal with.

She hoped if it all came to light it wouldn't put out that spark forever. She'd never forgive herself—or Glen, if it came to that.

Robey leveled her gaze at the preacher. "Thomas," she announced, "we need to talk."

CHAPTER 36

LOY

Friday afternoon, October 15, 2010

Miss Laura was back again.

Loy felt for Glen's note in his back pocket.

He sat on his haunches next to Rebel. If he stayed down like this beside the hound, he could keep him quiet. And she'd never see them way up here in the woods.

She went in the house with Momma. He should go put the note on her car.

He was about to stand up when he heard a low, warning growl a ways up the hill.

Loy sunk back down and stayed put. Rebel tucked his tail and whined. They must've sat that way for nigh onto an hour.

Finally, the front door opened and Miss Laura came out and got in her car. She pulled away awful fast.

Loy stood and looked around. All was quiet now. He took Rebel to the house then.

That's when he saw Momma's family albums on the table. The red one was open to a picture of Curry's place.

Loy didn't think that was a good thing. He made Rebel stay this time. He'd take the four-wheeler. He had to get there fast.

CHAPTER 37

LAURA

Friday, late afternoon, October 15, 2010

Laura turned onto route 194 toward Lansing and slowed her pace. She didn't want to miss the road sign. It should be a left. The GPS map showed it to the south side.

She passed a sign for Lansing and just afterwards spotted Buck Tail Lane. Laura slowed as she checked her mirrors and the road ahead, thankful there was no one else in sight.

She drove slowly down the rutted dirt lane, staying on the high grassy humps as much as possible. The Jeep wasn't loud, maybe her approach would go unnoticed. She didn't intend to stay unnoticed, but she wanted time to look around before she was confronted by anyone.

Laura had gone about a mile or so when she rounded a bend and spotted the trailer off to the right. There was a large parking area and a patch of sparse grass to its far right with a picnic table.

The driveway widened out and ran all the way back to a shed about fifty feet or so beyond the house. Laura took advantage of the flat, wide space to turn the Jeep around and face the road out just in case.

Forest and brush surrounded the place. It ran along both sides of the road on the way in and appeared to come right up to the back of the trailer. The road itself ended in the driveway, but Big Horse Creek wasn't far beyond that shed according to Beulah. Laura guessed there was a trail to it back there somewhere.

She turned toward the mobile home and studied it for a moment. Someone had kept the bulk of it painted. There was matching skirting underneath, but a few of the panels were open, or missing.

Laura climbed the steps and knocked. No one answered and there was no sound from inside. She knocked a second time. When no one came she tried the door knob. It turned.

She stuck her head in and called out, "Hello? Anybody home? Don't mean to intrude, but I'm here to see Curry Porter," Laura continued in a shaky voice as she stepped inside. "Hello? The door was open. I just need to talk to you. Please, if you're here, come out." She stood and looked around. It was silent.

The place wasn't spotless, but it wasn't as bad as she might have thought. There were old afghans draped over the furniture. Magazines lay out on the coffee table neatly stacked. The dark brown curtains looked old, but they appeared to be clean enough. The rug had a darkened path worn in it from constant traffic, though it did look like it had been vacuumed.

She could see into the kitchen to the right. There were coffee cups in the sink, but no piles of dirty dishes or rotting food anywhere. Not what she'd call pristine, but kept after, at least.

Somehow that surprised her. She just couldn't picture Curry Porter as a neat housekeeper. Not if his own clothes were any indication.

She glanced around nervously before she headed back the hall. There was a small bedroom to the right just big enough for the bed, a dresser and a chest of drawers with a little space to walk around them. The closet door was partly open and a man's coat hung from a hook inside. There was a pair of black dress shoes in the bottom.

The bed was made, the clothing all put away, nothing on the floor. The dresser top was a little cluttered with what appeared to be a man's things—a watch, a wallet and a few other odds and ends.

Laura continued down the hall and came to a small bathroom. It was narrow and the sink and toilet were both on one side of the room with a tub-shower across the end. Towels hung neatly on the shower bar and wall rack. A toothbrush, shaving cream and a razor were lined up along the sink edge.

The last bedroom on the end, the master bedroom, was a different story. Clothing lay in heaps on the floor. There was dust a quarter-inch thick on the dresser, the carpet was dirty, and the curtains tattered and falling down. It had its own small bathroom, but this one was filthy. The sink and toilet looked like they hadn't been cleaned in ages. There was trash laying around and dirty clothes and towels in the floor. And it stank.

It was clear there were two men living here. Two very different men.

Laura turned and headed back toward the living room. But as she passed the first bedroom again she recalled the dress shoes. She couldn't resist a closer look.

She opened the closet door and picked them up, turning them over and back. She'd seen them before, or a pair like them. The slight heel, the black polished shine, just like her father used to— wear. The thought caught her up short. Could it be a coincidence?

Laura set the shoes back in place and checked around the room further. She didn't dare root through the drawers. But as she considered the thought, something nearly out of sight on the bottom of the nightstand caught her eye.

It was a small picture frame. She went around the bed and reached down for the photo. She recognized the man and the small girl. As she set the picture back in place she heard a loud crack from somewhere outside.

Laura froze and held her breath, waiting for more. Seconds later it came again.

She hurried to the door and peeked out. There was no one in sight. She slipped out and made her way along the front of the trailer, staying close to the wall as the sound came again, clearer now from the direction of the shed. Whoever it was must not have seen the Jeep yet, or they'd have been the one sneaking up on her.

Thwack! The sound made her jump this time. She worked her way around the side of the shed.

Laura peered around the corner just as the sound rang out a fourth time. It was followed by a hacking cough. A man was doubled over next to a stump with a hatchet stuck in it. From what she could tell he was thin and the coughing had taken over his body for the moment.

When it finally stopped, he stood, his back to her. He was tall and very thin indeed. He took a handkerchief out of his pocket and wiped his mouth, then folded it over and wiped his brow. Suddenly he went still. After a pause, his head slowly turned toward her.

Laura could tell it wasn't Curry Porter. As much as she wanted to see the man's face she knew she ought to jump in the Jeep and go get the sheriff. But she was locked in place, unable to move a muscle. Reason told her if he was who she thought he was, he wouldn't hurt her.

Glen Porter finally turned to face her. He was pale and ghastly grey in the face, and much, much older. But it was her father.

Laura was about to reach out to him when she was stopped short by none other than Loy Porter, inches away. He gave her a look that was both angry and sad.

"T...t...tol' you—t...tol' you—Go home!" he demanded as he pointed his finger at her face. "Don' b'long *here!*" He said the last word with emphasis, then reached into his pocket and pulled out a crumpled piece of paper.

Before Laura could react, Glen Porter stepped up behind her, "Now Loy, quit tryin' to scare the girl. Gimme that note. I'll take care of her now. Won't no harm come, I promise. You go on. Go inside and wait." He glanced around quickly. "You didn't bring that old hound dog, did you?" His face was solemn and sad. "Cain't have him howlin' his head off or gettin' killed if . . ." but her father never finished the thought.

Loy shook his head. His eyes got big and he looked from Glen to Laura and back again. Something had him scared, but he did what his brother told him to. When he was out of sight, Glen took her by the shoulders and stared at her in silence.

"Oh, my sweet Laurie Allen. Thought I'd never get to see you again. My own baby girl, all growed up." He sounded proud, but his face was somber. "Wish I coulda . . ." his voice trailed off as a haunted look came over him. He turned away, then signaled her to follow. He led her into the shed. "We can talk in here without nobody seein' or hearin' us," he explained.

Twilight had begun to settle over the mountains and it was dim inside the building. He flipped a light on over a tall, simple work table made of plywood. There was sawdust and a few tools laying on top of it. The place smelled of wood dust and paint thinner like a carpenter's shop.

She looked around as her eyes adjusted to the light. There were projects everywhere in various stages of completion. Shelves full of hand-carved birds and animals, some painted, some not. Larger carved statues of owls, eagles, bears. Handmade, wood-burned picture frames and signs, even small tables, chairs and stands, some with mountain scenes carved into them.

Laura caught her breath and put a hand to her chest. "These are . . . beautiful," she finished softly as she ran a hand over the form of a red-tailed hawk sitting on the table.

As she looked up, she caught the first hint of a smile on her father's face. But he was suddenly overcome by another attack. When he straightened she was sure she saw blood on the handkerchief he used, just before he tucked it away.

"Did you make these?" she asked, motioning around the room.

"Yep. I like to make things with my hands. Wood's just about the best thing God ever created. It can be made into most anythin' you'd ever want or need. Yields to knife, saw, hammer, hatchet, and fire in ways nothin' else will."

His expression lifted as he talked about his hobby.

"I make this stuff to sell. Curry takes 'em round to Lansing, and to Grassy Creek, even Asheville, Cherokee, and Greensboro sometimes. Tourists like 'em for some reason. Cur collects the money for me. Takes 'em more. Gets my supplies. I cut the wood out here m'self when I can. Keeps body and soul together, an' a roof over our heads." He struggled to clear his throat then. "An' it's prob'ly what keeps me, uh, settled. Clear in my mind most a the time. Sometimes I work out here day and night, lose track a time. But that ain't what you come here to find out. An' it ain't what I need to tell you 'bout."

His body was wracked again by the hacking. His face grew so red she wondered how he could breath. He tried to stand but passed out and went down. In spite of how thin he was, Laura couldn't manage to get him up alone. She ran to the trailer, startling Loy when she burst in, but he understood what was wrong and came to help. They got Glen into his bed and Laura got a cool rag.

There was something seriously wrong with her father. She asked Loy if they had any medicine for him or if he knew what to do. He handed her a bottle of smelling salts. That brought her father around, but his color had turned greyer and a bluish tinge crept in around the edges of his eyes and mouth.

Glen looked up at her and whispered, "Laurie, you got to sit down here beside me. There's things I gotta tell you. Loy, go get me some water and one a them kitchen chairs for Laurie." Glen patted his brother's hand and encouraged him, "Go on now. It'll be all right."

Loy came back with the chair first and returned with the water a minute later. They helped Glen sit partway up, stacking pillows behind him. He took a couple of light sips and laid his head back as his eyelids drooped. Loy left the room.

Laura thought Glen must have drifted off to sleep, but his eyes finally opened again with a faraway look. He traveled through time in his memory—she could see it in his face. That open-eyed distant look that meant a person was somewhere else.

"When your momma told me she was pregnant with you, it liked to scare me to death," his voice was barely above a whisper. "Then I had to marry Callie, but I loved your momma. I'd been with her before Callie ever come along. I was wrackin' my brain tryin' to figure a way outta things. A way I could be with your momma and the little one that was comin'. I wanted to, Laurie. I wanted to awful bad."

His eyes implored her to believe in his love.

"I just got so frustrated with it all. I took off again, like I always did when I couldn't face things. Took Loy and Curry with me. Went to work in the tobacco fields out in Lowgap."

He broke off to cough and clear his throat. Laura helped him get another sip of water.

"Made a good bit a money. Thought I'd have enough to take you and your momma and get out of North Carolina maybe. But the more I thought about it, the more I knew I couldn't get out of my marriage to Callie. It'd be wrong to do that, too." He stopped and coughed hard again, hacking into his handkerchief.

His eyes watered, he closed them tight against the tears. But he breathed easier at last and went on. "I was feelin' angered about it all, so we stopped by Johnny Bean's for a bottle a moonshine on our way home that weekend. Me and Curry anyway. Loy never drank the stuff, and I drank it way too often. I gave it up a few years ago. Been better since, but I know I ain't got long.

"I been wrong 'bout a lotta things. But I got control a most of 'em. 'Cept them damn cigarettes. Guess they're killin' me. Them an' the beast. It got a hold on me long ago. I ain't gettin' away with what I done." He peered intently at Laura then.

She felt uncomfortable, but she had to know.

"What beast are you talking about? You were always so sweet to me and Momma. I don't understand, Daddy," she pleaded for him to explain.

He went into another coughing fit. When it stopped he slumped into the pillows and closed his eyes again. She waited, not sure what to do. Suddenly he opened them wide, staring hard at the ceiling like he saw something she couldn't. He raised his hands to shield his face and moaned.

"I cain't. I cain't say it. I thought I could tell you myself, but I just cain't do it, Laurie. I wrote it down in case I couldn't bring myself to say it out loud. The papers," he pointed his thumb weakly over his shoulder. "I hid 'em under the bed. Slit a piece of carpet under the headboard and stuffed 'em under."

Laura stretched up and looked down into the space between the wall and the bed.

"You take 'em Laurie and hide 'em. Don't let that beast find 'em . . . and don't let Loy or Curry find out about 'em either. Then you gotta get outta here. Take 'em and go, girl. It's gettin' late, no tellin' when he'll be back." He grasped her arm as he talked, but his grip was weak.

Laura started to get down to look at the carpet when Glen was overcome by another coughing fit. Loy came and stood in the doorway watching. Glen looked into her eyes, imploring her to hurry. But she didn't want to leave him like this. Not when she'd just found him again. Not when he was so obviously in need of medical help.

"I can take you to the hospital. Or at least to a doctor," she offered hopefully.

Loy turned on her, anger in his face, shaking his head. "No!" he barked out clearly. "You go—now!" he demanded.

Glen shook his head, too. "No, Laurie, he's comin'. Loy's right. You gotta get outta here. He's close." He turned just enough to look at his little brother. "Loy, you go keep an eye out." Loy turned into the hall. Glen looked back to her. "Be quick now," he urged.

In the next instant, a low guttural growl began outside the window. Then Laura heard an engine roar to a stop in the driveway. Heavy footfalls sounded on the porch steps and the trailer door banged open with a shatter of glass.

CHAPTER 38

CURRY

Friday evening, October 15, 2010

"Whose God-damned Jeep is that in my yard?" Curry Porter's eyes burned yellow-amber.

He sniffed the air. Glen's girl was in his house. He growled deep and angry.

"Got no business bein' here. Now you're gonna pay."

Curry's chest swelled and his head came up. His fists clenched and unclenched the cold steel he held in his hands. The beast was near. He could always count on its strength at the moment he needed it. It was time they showed little miss high-and-mighty what happens to outsiders who come snooping around their mountains.

Curry's eyes burned hotter and he felt a surge of power like a massive electrical charge run through him.

CHAPTER 39

LAURA

Friday evening, October 15, 2010

Loy's face went white as the pillowcases behind Glen's head as he slunk backwards, cowering against the wall as Curry crashed through the living room. In the next instant Curry blocked the doorway, rifle held tight in both hands, the barrel aimed into the room.

The man literally growled like an animal. "What in hell you doin' here?" he demanded as he stared Laura down.

"Cur," Glen interrupted in a weak voice, "she just came to see her daddy. You let her be, you hear me?"

The man's eyes blazed and he reeked of whiskey. He looked for all the world like a demon about to cut loose. All his focus was centered on her. She had to get out somehow. But another growl echoed from outside. Curry's head snapped up as he looked toward the window.

"You shouldn't a called her here, Glen. You know what's out there and it's gonna smell her out quick," Curry snarled. "Your little girl's bound to get hurt," he said with deliberation.

Suddenly there was a loud knock at the front door. "Curry Porter, you in there? I need to talk to you." The voice was Tom Honeywell's.

Laura drew in a sharp breath and glanced at the open doorway.

"We're not here to make trouble, Curry. I just came to get my daughter and we'll be on our way." And Robey. *How on earth did they know she was here?*

Laura tried to think fast as she eyed the gun in Curry's hand and listened for the growl outside. She glanced at his face then. Some of the fire had gone out of him. He looked from Laura to Loy, and back at Glen. His lips curled in an ugly sneer.

"They ain't takin' me," he snarled in a low voice. "They can have you if you want it that way. It was all your fault anyhow, Glen. You know that. You mark my words. I ain't gonna be taken in by them."

Before she could move, Curry grabbed Laura by the arm and yanked her in front of him. He gripped the gun in his right hand, pressing it against her back, pushing her forward out of the room.

Somehow Glen summoned the strength to jump out of the bed and grab Curry from behind, breaking his hold on her. Loy shrank to the floor and curled into a ball.

Laura's feet got tangled up in Curry's and she went down. She heard her mother scream. Tom yelled something as she fell backward and hit her head on the dresser. She was dazed but somehow held onto consciousness. When she looked up, she saw Curry had turned the gun on her.

Tom rushed in just as Glen lunged in front of Laura. Tom grabbed the gun and yanked it free but not before a shot rang out—and Glen fell back onto Laura's legs.

Curry was no match for the preacher. He wriggled loose and was about to run when Tom caught him with a right hook and the older man went down, hard. He appeared to be out cold.

"Oh, my god. Laura, are you okay? Were you hit?" Robey pushed her way into the room and knelt beside her daughter, tears beginning to flow.

Tom turned to help Glen, but he wasn't moving. His face had gone pale, his lips were blue and blood seeped through his shirt front. Laura pulled her legs out from under him and scrambled forward with Tom, who had knelt to check their father's pulse.

He shook his head sadly. "I'm sorry, Laura. He's gone."

Before she could react, Loy let out a scream. He was shivering and shaking his head. He sat rocking himself, arms crossed in front of him, tears running down his cheeks as he pointed.

"No, no, no, no, no, no, no," he mumbled, "it ain' over. It ain' over."

They all followed his gaze. Curry had disappeared.

Loy sunk back into a fetal position on the floor, shaking his head and repeating, "It ain' over, it ain' over, it ain' over." His eyes were squeezed shut, hands clasped under his chin.

Tom glanced around the room. A sigh escaped him as he looked back at his father slumped on the floor. "Guess I better call the sheriff," he said flatly.

He pulled out his phone and started to make the call. He shook his head and glared at it. Then he stepped out of the room, presumably to try again. Laura could hear him mumbling as he slapped the phone shut.

"Damn!" the preacher swore. "Either of you have a cell phone with you?"

Laura pulled hers out but she had no service either.

"Okay," he drew a breath, "Robey, you take my car. Go into Lansing and call Sheriff Wilson. I'll stay here with Laura . . . just in case."

Robey took Tom's keys as they exchanged a knowing glance. Her mother nodded almost imperceptibly, but Laura saw it. She was confused.

Robey stopped briefly to kneel beside Glen's body. She smoothed his hair back and laid her palm gently against his cheek. "I hope you're free now," she whispered as a tear dripped from her chin to land on his shirt sleeve.

When she stood and looked back at Laura, Robey didn't say a word. Her eyes pleaded for patience and understanding. Then she turned and left.

Tom tried to get Loy to calm down. He reassured him help was on the way and things would be all right. But their uncle just kept mumbling.

The preacher tried to help him to his feet. Loy grabbed Tom's shirt front and shouted, "N...N...No! You don' u...un...un...unerstan', it AIN' OVER!"

Laura stood carefully, testing her balance.

At that instant, something behind the trailer scraped the aluminum siding with an awful screech. The growl started, again, low and deep like an animal—a wolf maybe—but different. It sounded human and animal at the same time.

Laura's head snapped up. It was the same sound she'd heard in the woods before. And, she realized suddenly, the same sound she'd heard in her dreams.

She exchanged a wide-eyed look with Tom. He'd heard it too. It wasn't her imagination. But his expression turned grim. His lips drew together in a tight line and his shoulders rose and fell as he let out a determined sigh.

"Tom?" Laura sought his face. Whatever was out there, he didn't seem surprised by it.

Loy shrunk back against the opposite wall, drawing his shoulders in and pointing toward the sound. "I...I...I tol'...I tol' you," he whispered this time.

Tom went to the closet, searching for something as the sound moved around the trailer. It was headed toward the front.

"Thank God," Tom declared as he rummaged through the shelf above and pulled out a box of cartridges. The preacher quickly loaded the gun and chambered a round, then made sure the safety was on.

He handed the weapon to Laura while he coaxed Loy into the closet and shut the door. It wasn't hard to do. Loy crawled into the furthest corner and curled up, head down on his knees as if he could fold in on himself and disappear.

Taking the gun back, Tom tried to get Laura to join Loy but she refused. "You might need help," she urged. "And he—it—will only come in here looking for us if it gets by you."

Tom sighed, "You sure are a stubborn woman." He shook his head and put a finger to his lips.

The growling and scraping stopped. Someone pounded up the front steps. Tom motioned for Laura to follow. They slipped down the hallway to the back door. He whispered for her to grab the knob and get ready to open it when he signaled.

The front door smashed open. More glass showered the room. "Now!" Tom yelled. "Go, go! Land and run!"

He pushed her from behind as Laura threw the door open and jumped. She hadn't noticed there were no steps back here until that instant. The height wasn't that much, but it had been unexpected. She got the wind knocked out of her when she landed, leaving her dazed for a moment.

Quickly, she got to her feet and turned to look for Tom. He hadn't followed.

The door was shut, and he hadn't followed.

Laura looked toward the front door. There was no movement there but the screen door stood open, its upper hinges snapped.

Tom had told her to run, *but he was supposed to follow to draw the thing back outside*, she thought. She couldn't leave him to face the creature alone.

The sound of snarling and growling reached her again. There was a sudden yelp, like a wounded animal. Then a loud angry howl.

Laura ran back for the door she'd come out of. She managed to pull it open at the bottom, though she couldn't reach the knob. She peeked in. Tom was locked in a struggle with someone, or something. She heard him grunt and cry out in pain.

He managed the words, "In the name of God, you devil. You—go—back—where—you—came—from." Then her brother's body went slack.

Laura spied the rifle on the floor a few feet away. She shimmied up on her belly as the creature shook Tom's limp form in the air. She raised up on one knee and slid the gun into the crook of her shoulder. Flipping the safety off, she took aim.

Just like a target, she told herself. *Pick your bullseye.*

As the thing lowered Tom's body to look her way, she found her mark. She aimed for the throat and squeezed the trigger.

Tom slid from the creature's grasp to the floor as it glared at her in disbelief. Flaring red-rimmed eyes dimming, it—no he—staggered back. It grabbed its neck with one hand, then turned and took off as Laura scrambled to her feet.

She slid the rifle bolt forward and back with a loud *kerchunk*. The spent round flew off into the thick shag carpet as another shell locked into place.

She headed after the thing that was Curry Porter, but not entirely him. By the time she got outside though, he'd disappeared. She looked all around, but there wasn't so much as a trace of him.

Laura listened for several long minutes in the dark heavy silence. The air was still—too still—no night birds singing, crickets chirping, nothing. A familiar tingle crawled up her neck and spread across her scalp. She turned then and rushed back inside to check on Tom.

"Oh, God, please let him be alive," she pleaded.

Her brother still lay on the floor where the beast had dropped him. He was on his side, his eyes closed, mouth slightly open. His arms, face and upper thighs were bleeding and he was awfully pale. Laura leaned down to check for a pulse and feel for his breath.

Tom moaned and Laura breathed a sigh of relief. *He's alive!* For the moment at least. Help would be coming soon. But blood was running thick and dark from his upper thigh. She looked around for something to staunch the flow.

Laura ripped a curtain to make a tourniquet and tied it in place above the gash. She was no medic but the wound looked deep. The curtains were clean enough, so she made a bandage out of what was left, tying it in place with gentle pressure. Then she went in search of anything else to administer first aid with.

She sobbed as she stepped past her father's still form. She recovered the smelling salts from his bedside nightstand. Then she remembered the written confession.

She glanced at the closet. "Loy," Laura called his name as she slowly pulled the door open.

But he was gone. He must have slipped out the back.

She quickly pulled her father's bed away from the wall. The carpet didn't look like it was slit anywhere. She went back to the end of the bed and pulled harder, dragging it far enough for her to fit her whole body behind the headboard.

Laura got down then and crawled forward slowly, running her hands along the rug surface till she found it. Under the flap of carpet was a manila envelope with her name on it. She opened it and found a sheaf of notebook papers stapled together. She shoved them back in the envelope and closed the fastener. Then she folded it all in half and stuffed it in the back of her pants, covering it with both shirts.

He'd told her not to let the beast find the envelope, but the beast was gone now. Maybe even dead, or dying, out there in the woods somewhere. Still, she felt compelled to keep the envelope and its contents hidden—for now at least.

Laura pushed the bed back in place. She knelt by her father. Touched his hand, she whispered, "I'll tell them the truth." Then she hurried back to the living room to wait with Tom.

She kept the gun close and her ears tuned as she held her brother's hand and tried to get him to come around.

Laura's whole body tensed and her head came up instantly when she heard the sound of gravel crunching under tires. But when she saw the flashing lights, she relaxed.

Seconds later, Blaine Wilson called out, "Tom? Laura? This is Sheriff Wilson. You two okay?"

She called back, "We're inside. I'm okay, but Tom's hurt bad. It's just us in here."

He called out again, "Coming in."

She could hear his carefully placed footsteps as he climbed the porch. He had to duck to get through the trailer door, and he came in gun drawn. But he lowered the weapon slowly as he took in the scene at a glance. He looked down then as broken glass crunched under his boots.

"What the hell happened in here?" he asked.

Laura hadn't paid much attention to anything other than her brother's condition till then. But she followed Blaine's gaze now. There were holes scraped into the carpet like claw marks. The couch stuffing hung out where it had been slashed. And there was blood spatter everywhere. The room looked like a war zone.

She shook her head, eyes wide as Sheriff Wilson bent over Tom, checking for vital signs.

"I shot him," Laura blurted out.

The sheriff looked up, his green eyes piercing hers.

"I shot Curry," she clarified her statement. "He attacked Tom. I shot him in the throat. He disappeared."

"You did a good job with that tourniquet. You just might've saved his life. There's an ambulance on the way." Sheriff Wilson patted her shoulder, gently taking the rifle from her. "It'll be all right, Laura. You were just trying to save your brother."

A siren blipped and more flashing lights illuminated the room. The sheriff stepped out the door to call the paramedics in, then turned back to Laura again.

He bent down to her level. "Laura," he said her name softly, in spite of the dark frown on his face. "They're taking you both to the hospital. I have to get out there to direct things. There's a few more departments coming. Your momma seemed to think we'd need someone from animal control. Something about a big wolf with sharp claws. You have any idea what she's talking about?" Blaine Wilson looked her in the eye and waited.

Laura opened her mouth to speak but the room started to spin. All at once she felt like she was hearing him through a tunnel, or a fog, and he was getting further away. Then everything went dark and she crumpled to the floor.

CHAPTER 40

CURRY

Friday night, October 15, 2010

Curry Porter ran like a wounded animal at first. She'd shot him. That upstart girl from Pennsylvania had shot him in the neck! There was blood on his hands and shirt, but he was sure it wasn't all his own.

He remembered a struggle with someone. A man, Glen's boy, Tom. Curry hoped he hadn't hurt him. Tom was a good enough fella, he didn't deserve to get hurt because of that bitch child his daddy sent away years ago.

Curry stopped at the stream and tore off his shirt. He used it as a bandage to stop the flow for the time being. It would heal. He always healed up pretty good. That was something else he got from the beast. That and the strength of a man less than half his age— at least while they were joined.

His mind was clearing now. He couldn't go back again. Glen was dead, he had to figure a way to make it on his own. He couldn't contact his momma anymore either.

The creature was his only companion now. Maybe that's what it wanted all along.

CHAPTER 41

LAURA

Friday night, October 15, 2010

When Laura woke up in the ambulance on her way to the hospital, she felt for the envelope tucked in the back of her pants.

"Hey there, guess you got a worse knock on the noggin' than you thought." From a fold-out seat at the back of the ambulance, Robey cupped a thin, blue-veined hand over Laura's blanketed foot.

"Hey, Mom, where were you? I don't remember seeing you with Blaine."

"Oh, so it's Blaine now, is it?" Robey's tone made Laura blush. "Well, I was outside in '*Blaine's*' patrol car, waiting to see if you needed me."

When Laura responded with raised eyebrows, her mother went on, "I told him this is about family, my family. I wasn't about to stay behind. He seemed to understand."

Laura closed her eyes against the pain in her head, but she gave a weak, crooked grin as she mumbled, "Hmm. Did they find Curry? Or that—that thing, yet?"

Robey averted her gaze, dropped her head and didn't speak at first. When she did, she wouldn't look at Laura. She shrugged her shoulders and replied, "You know as much as I do." Then she sighed as she folded her hands in her lap and studied them, "But I doubt it. They probably never will."

Laura shook her head, "But I shot him in the neck. I saw the blood. He grabbed his throat with one hand and ran out. He couldn't have gone far with that kind of wound."

Laura watched her mother's face.

"You knew about this, didn't you?" She accused more than asked. "And Tom, did he know, too? What's going on? Was that Curry I shot, or some...thing else?"

Laura had forgotten about the paramedics until her mother glanced at them nervously. She saw Robey's silent plea for her to let the conversation drop. Laura laid her head back then and closed her eyes until they pulled into the hospital.

They didn't keep her long. The attending doctor told her to take an over-the-counter pain reliever for the headache and use ice. He advised her to take it easy for a day or two. No strenuous exercise or lifting, but assured her she would be fine.

The sheriff met them in the waiting room. Eyebrows drawn, Blaine Wilson heaved a sigh before he spoke, "How's the patient doing?"

Laura glanced up at him then dropped her gaze to her hands, "I'm fine. Just a slight concussion. But what about Tom? Is he all right?" She barely got the question out when the preacher's wife, Elizabeth, rushed in.

The sheriff took Elizabeth's arm and helped her to a seat as he spoke. "Tom's in rough shape, but he'll make it. They're stitching him up now and giving him blood. They'll be out to let you know when you can see him," he told her.

He must have felt the less said the better for now. He simply told the preacher's wife Tom had gone to Curry's trailer to ask him about Glen, and they'd got into an altercation.

Then he turned to Laura. His expression darkened. "I'm going to need to talk to you and your mother. But I've got to get back out there right now. Go home and get some rest. I'll come by tomorrow morning around 8:30 or so."

As he put his hat on he added, "Oh, and your Jeep is outside. I had one of the deputies bring it over, but you better let Robey drive."

"It's a stick shift," Laura replied.

"And is that supposed to mean I can't drive it?" Robey asked sarcastically. "I was driving stick before you were born."

Laura just looked at her then. *Wonders never cease.*

They waited long enough to see Tom before heading back to Aunt Hattie's. The two barely spoke on the drive. Laura laid her head back and put the ice pack on top. Robey seemed content with the silence, as usual.

When they got back, she turned to Laura, "I know you have questions. But Sheriff Wilson is right. You need to get some rest. I'll check on you after while. We can talk tomorrow."

Laura was too tired and achy to argue. She went up to her room. But as she undressed she pulled out the envelope. In all the rush she'd forgotten about it. She slipped on a nightshirt, crawled in bed, and pulled out the papers.

It was written in neat tiny rows between the lines. The print was tight and small, and so close together it was difficult to pick out the word breaks at first. It went on for four and a half pages in plain blue ink. Mistakes and rewrites were simply crossed out and reworded, as if Glen Porter had just kept writing until he had nothing else to say.

Laura paused and stared at the blue lines, not reading at first. Did she want to know what could have caused her father to abandon them all those years ago, sending the woman he loved and their child off away from him forever?

But she had come back here to find the truth. And she still wanted to know. He was gone now. She'd never be able to restore the relationship she'd missed. Now it was time she knew why.

By the time she'd finished reading, spidery fingers of fear ran up her spine. She couldn't help but get up to look out the window. The night was dark, moonless and quiet, yet she couldn't shake the sense of dread that crept over her.

Laura went back to bed and read the confession again—over and over—trying to understand how her loving father could have been part of something so unspeakably horrible.

How could the same hands that had tossed her playfully in the air as a child—the same hands that held her safely on her daddy's lap when he came to visit, the same hands that had crafted those beautiful works of art with wood since then—have done something so utterly evil? As she fell asleep, her father's confession played like a horror movie in her mind.

In her dreams she saw the wolf man/beast as it prowled the woods, seeking to ravage the innocent blue-eyed girl. The air was still and muggy, the sky darkened ominously. As the child hid herself in the trees, Laura became one with her again. The beast growled and sniffed the air, wandering back and forth searching. She could smell its stink and feel its harsh breath. It was close.

She was small and no longer wore the blue dress. It had rotted off. But then there wasn't much of her left either. She was only bones with no skin. Her dolly was faded and ugly now. Then it was day again, though she couldn't see it well from where she was. She just knew it wasn't dark out beyond.

And then there was another little girl. The one who'd crawled in looking for something when she'd bumped into her skeleton.

It was Laura, she was herself again, but now she was seven years old, looking into the sunken holes in Lottie Edwards' skull. And then she saw them—the other little girl's clear-blue slanted eyes. They pleaded for her to help.

Then she was bones again, and suddenly it was daylight. So bright she had to shut her eyes. As if she hadn't seen the sun in a very long time. There was a man who was pulling her body from under the porch. Now the other little girl who'd found her was no longer there.

Laura floated through dreamtime, herself once again, kneeling by Lottie Edwards' grave. The stone was clean. She could feel its cool surface as she ran her fingers across the name engraved there.

She tossed and turned as the dream faded and came back several times in the night. Each time she changed roles. Alternately she felt the fear and desolation of the little girl who'd been abused so badly and left to the elements for years, and her own fear and confusion when she'd found the skull and somehow glimpsed the frightened, tortured soul of Lottie Edwards.

CHAPTER 42

GLEN

Thursday night, September 1, 1960

The moonshine went down like fire but it gave a man a big feeling. Glen was enjoying the sensation when he heard Curry taunting Loy.

"Hey Loy, what's goin' on with you and that crazy Lottie Edwards? I see you two always together."

Curry gave Glen a sneering grin over his shoulder as he took another swig of 'shine. Finger hooked in the jug's handle, his sharp yellowed eye-teeth glittered in the moonlight. Glen figured he was brewing up some awful idea in that twisted mind of his. Curry was known to have a mean streak. He was also known to use it on his younger brother to torment him when the mood struck. And the moonshine was a mood striker for sure.

Loy ducked his head and fell back a few paces. Glen knew he understood the insinuations in Curry's voice well enough.

"Hey, hey," his voice slurred, "you know what I heard? I heard her momma and daddy had her down to Raleigh for one a them op'rations to keep her from gettin' pregnant. You know, that ster-i-li-za-tion," Curry dragged the word out, pronouncing one syllable at a time.

"You know what that means, don'tcha Loy? Means no matter how much a feller pokes at her, she ain't gonna have no pups from it," Curry snorted with laughter. "Yep, it's a free pass for a feller, that's what it is."

He leaned in close to Glen, passing the bottle back to him as he winked. Glen grabbed the jug by its handle and eyed his brother in the moonlight.

Loy dragged his feet and drifted further back but followed on.

"Now come on, Cur, they ain't no reason to go embarrassin' the boy. It's pure and natural those two'd be attracted to each other." Glen got caught up in the teasing for the moment. "Why, fact is, they're plum perfect for each other. Loy can't help it he don't know nothin' 'bout females," Glen snickered and slapped Curry's back.

"Your girl's house is just up the road a piece, ain't it?" Curry asked Loy. "You know which window is hers?"

Glen returned Curry's 'follow my lead' stare that morphed into an eerie smirk in the dim light. Loy ducked his chin to his chest and pulled his shoulders in, but Glen and Curry took up place on either side of him, each with a hand on his shoulder.

"C'mon Loy boy, let's go check out your girl's place. See if she can come out an' play with us a while," Curry took hold of Loy's arm and winked over his head at Glen again. Glen grabbed Loy's other arm then as they half dragged him along to speed him up.

By the time they got close to the house, Loy had slacked his whole weight against them, dragging his feet. They stopped and dropped him to the ground a few yards away in the treeline behind the small story-and-a-half clapboard.

Glen staggered as they did, not from Loy's weight, but from the effects of the moonshine. They'd polished off the entire bottle.

Loy continued to lay where he'd fallen.

"Go on, Loy. Go get your girl. We'll all go down to the pond and catch us some frogs," Curry urged in a hard whisper as he tossed a few pebbles randomly at a window.

Turned out he hit the right one. Lottie's full fair face appeared as Loy drew himself up in front of Glen and Curry. Of course she couldn't see who was out there in the dark, but the girl opened the window and stuck her head out, calling softly to the only person she would expect to be there.

"Oy?" she called in a loud whisper. "Da oo?"

"Yea. I here La-ee," Loy answered, his voice stifled.

"I comeen'," she called back just before she disappeared from view.

The moonlight reflected bright off her pale blue dress as Lottie reappeared, crawling awkwardly across the sill. She lowered herself to a rock beneath the window and hopped down onto the grass. Her feet padded the ground in soft thuds.

Curry took her arm before Loy could, and they turned down the path to the pond. Glen fell into step with them.

Lottie gave Glen a quizzical look. He turned a reassuring smile on her and nodded hello. She smiled back, then turned her attention to the path at her feet. Glen knew she'd made this trek many times before with Loy, but she still walked gingerly, like she had to plan each step.

Curry reached behind Lottie and grabbed Glen's arm, tugging him over to walk beside him. He whispered his plan to Glen, then began to pull the girl off the beaten path.

"You know, Lottie, I really been wantin' to talk to you for a long time. You're such a sweet young thing and old Loy there's been occupyin' all your time. So I was wonderin' if you'd take to spendin' some time with me out here in the moonlight."

Lottie looked up at him as he steered her off into the trees. Loy lunged toward them but Glen grabbed for him. "Hold on there, little brother. They're just gonna get to know each other a bit. You and me just gonna wait here while they do."

Loy strained against Glen as the sound of Lottie's frightened grunts and protests reached them. When she screamed outright, he twisted hard and ducked under Glen's arm. He broke free and darted into the trees calling Lottie's name. Glen headed after him hot on his heels.

The fractured moonlight glanced off Curry's bare backside as they stumbled upon him huddled over top of Lottie. She screamed and cried and pummeled him with her small white fists clenched tight.

Glen grabbed Loy again, this time in a cradle-hold on both arms. Loy tugged and fought but Glen refused to let go. The two stood and watched as Curry did the awful thing. Glen froze, eyes wide like a startled deer while Loy hung his head and whimpered like a whooped pup.

Lottie opened her hands and clawed at Curry's back but he grabbed them and slammed both her arms to the ground until he was done. When he went slack though, she pushed up under him kicking, biting and scratching again.

Curry hauled back hard with his right fist and smashed her in the face this time. Glen watched, mesmerized. She made a gurgling sound and tried to scream. That's when Curry raised up and pummeled her with both fists.

Coming to his senses at last, Glen jumped in and grabbed his brother's wrists to stop the flailing. "Cur, dammit man, stop it. You're gonna kill her, goddammit!"

Lottie suddenly went quiet and still. Glen and Curry stood over her, the milky moonlight reflecting off the blood running down her face. Loy dropped to the ground, head in his hands as he rocked his upper body and moaned.

"Goddammit, Curry," Glen swore, "what'd you do? Is she breathin'?"

"W...w...w...whadaya mean? Sure she's breathin'. I um . . ." Curry's voice slurred as he sat back on his heels. He gaped at Lottie's still form. His eyes went wide and over-bright, his mouth hanging open. Finally, he slumped forward and pushed off the ground with both hands, hiking his britches up as he stood. Then he gawked at his own hands and tried to wipe the blood and dirt off.

About that time, Loy let out a high-pitched soulful wail. "Noooooooo!"

Glen ran to him, knocked him down, jumped on him, and covered his mouth. "Somebody's gonna hear you. Shut up, you dumb retard," he declared in a loud whispered growl.

Curry joined Glen, cuffing Loy hard alongside the head. Loy grabbed his ear and fell over, dissolving into quiet sobs as tears squeezed out from between his clenched eyelids.

That's when Lottie groaned. She was coming around, and she was making noise again. The sound froze both Glen and Curry in their tracks.

"Holy shit! She ain't dead yet. Do somethin', Glen," Curry pleaded, all sign of bravado gone out of him. "If anybody finds out what we done we'll be up shit creek."

"Damn you, Cur. If you hadn't a hit her we coulda just left her wander off. She couldn't a told nobody what happened," Glen declared, then he punched Curry in the stomach. "Dumbass! What do you want me to do about it?"

"I dunno, but you can't let 'em send me to prison. Momma'd die a sorrow and shame. Come on, Glen, help me. Do somethin'," Curry demanded with a pitiful grimace as he grabbed his abdomen with both hands and doubled over.

Glen looked at Loy sobbing on the ground and back at Curry whose eyes were wide and glassy. He barely glanced over Lottie who had gone quiet again for the moment.

But his gaze fell on a big rock laying nearby, and slowly, the terrible thought began to grow. He didn't want to. It scared the piss out of him. But it was there in his mind, beginning to swell in his brain like a tick filling with blood.

Curry stumbled over to where Glen stood. His eyes went wide and his mouth dropped open as he gawked at Glen.

There was no other choice. It would be the easiest way. It'd be like killing an unwanted animal. Smash it quick and hard and it would never know what hit it.

Glen finally made the move. He dragged his feet, scuffling toward the rock, gaze fixed on it the whole time. He dared not take his eyes off it lest it disappear and leave him with no option. Or worse yet, rear up with a life of its own and hammer him instead for his evil thoughts.

It was only inches from her head. He didn't have to look at her. He could just pick it up, raise it high, aim for the forehead, and smash.

It was done before he realized he had been the one to wield the blow. Lottie Edwards was surely dead this time.

Glen looked up at Curry, who had drawn in close to watch. He stared at Lottie, his face was white but there was a twisted sort of sneer to his mouth. And he actually licked his lips.

Then as if realizing he was being watched he jerked his gaze to Glen. The sneer changed in an instant. "What now, Glen?"

"What, nothin'. We beat it the hell out of here and never come back to this spot again."

Glen turned to grab Loy only to find he was gone. Somehow he had slipped away while they were occupied with the dreadful deed.

"Dammit, now we gotta find him and make sure he don't talk," Curry declared.

"He'll head home, you know that," Glen replied with an unnatural calm.

Glen looked at the rock on the ground beside Lottie's blonde hair. It had an evil, dark, wet glitter to it. They had to get rid of it, but now that the deed was done, he gagged and retched as he picked it up again.

It was cold to the touch, cold as death.

And when he tossed into the pond as they passed, Glen saw the eerie glow of two yellow-amber lights in the trees beyond.

CHAPTER 43

LAURA

Saturday, October 16, 2010

Laura woke to the sound of voices and the clanging of pots and pans below in the kitchen. She rolled over to check the clock. It was 7:15. She clambered out of bed and headed for the bathroom.

She studied herself in the mirror briefly. Her highlighted, shoulder-length brown hair was a frumpy mess and there were circles under her eyes. Still, Laura supposed fretful sleep was better than no sleep at all.

The headache was gone. But she was far from feeling up to par, and Blaine Wilson would be there in a little over an hour.

After she showered and dressed, she gathered the papers she'd left strewn on the bed—the pages of her father's horrible confession—and tucked them back into the envelope. She'd have to tell the sheriff about them. She should have given them to him at the hospital and never read the ghastly details.

The sheriff would take the confession for evidence. Truth was, she didn't care. She couldn't think of any reason she'd want to keep the evil story around. It was already burned into her memory anyway—and her dreams. Except now she could put the faces in them that had been missing.

She arrived downstairs just in time to hear the knock at the door. It had taken her longer to get ready than usual. She told herself it was because of the restless night.

Robey stepped into the sitting room but stopped when she saw Laura. Her mother gave her that raised eyebrow look, a tiny smirk playing at her lips. Then she turned on her heel and went back to the kitchen.

"Good morning," Blaine Wilson announced as he stepped through the doorway. Somehow everything in the room looked more feminine, smaller and more delicate in comparison to his presence.

He eyed her briefly, "How's your head?"

Laura held the folded manila envelope in one hand and closed the door behind him with the other as she answered, "My *head's* fine."

Blaine caught the intended subtlety, "You want to tell me about it? I'm guessing that envelope has something to do with what's not?"

"Breakfast's ready, you two," Aunt Hattie called. "Come on in here and put some food in your bellies before you get to talkin' serious stuff."

When they had finished their meal, Laura led the sheriff out onto the front porch. They sat down in a pair of rocking chairs and she held out the envelope to him.

"Now then, what's this all about?" he asked as he pulled the papers out, his expression grim.

"It's his confession," she stated flatly.

Blaine looked back up at her then and nodded, eyebrows raised, mouth pursed as though he'd expected as much. "This is evidence. Don't you think you should've told me about this last night?"

Laura dropped her head and sat back, rocking gently as Blaine read.

"You read this, I suppose?" He leveled his gaze at her when she nodded. "Well, I guess that settles it then," he said simply. "At least we know what happened to Lottie Edwards."

"What more do you want?" Laura looked up at him, eyebrows raised.

"We didn't find Curry anywhere. Followed a blood trail a ways, but it stopped suddenly. It got too dark to do anything more, and in case you hadn't noticed it rained hard in the night. Anything that might've still been traceable has been washed away. I don't see how any man, but especially a man his age, could get far with a neck wound like that."

Laura studied his face. "But what about the—beast—creature, whatever it was? Curry seemed to change—morph—I don't know. It was . . . scary."

"I don't know of any beast in these woods that can make a man go crazy enough to do what those boys did." Blaine Wilson scowled and shook his head. "I think when men do evil things, and then they realize they have, they look for someone or something else to blame it on. They claim to be crazy so the guilt doesn't eat them alive inside."

He propped both elbows on the rocking chair arms and looked down a minute. Then he snapped the envelope on his thigh. "I don't know. Maybe after enough years of believing in the power of something like that, they somehow conjured it up. Or at least maybe they thought so." He shrugged. "The preacher seems to think it's real for Curry anyway. Who knows?"

Laura wanted to tell him about the dreams, but his reaction to the creature caused her to hold her tongue.

"Oh yeah, Loy made it home to Beulah's last night. I dragged him out of bed this morning. Those notes you found were from him. He's been watching out for you ever since you got here." Blaine kept looking at her as he talked. It seemed he kept thinking of things to say. And he wore a constant scowl. "We'll keep looking for Curry. This confession is enough to bring him for questioning at least." Blaine looked at her intently then, his brow furrowed, his mouth set firm. "I won't give up the search. I can promise you that much. But I'm going to have to ask you not to get involved again. Leave this to the law."

He kept his eyes on her face as he spoke, his voice sharp, "You could've been killed last night."

Laura averted her gaze. But he paused so long, she finally looked up at him.

"Tom could've bled to death," he said. "And now a rape and murder suspect has gone to ground somewhere out there in those mountains, and I'm going to have to flush him out. You should think before you—" he finished with a heavy sigh.

Blaine lifted the envelope then smacked it against his other hand as he stood. "I'm going to speak to your mother a minute." He turned and reached for the screen door. "There'll be a funeral for your father, I suppose. Whatever you and Robey choose to do is fine. Won't be a crowd, but I'll come. Tom should be able to say a few words by then. He was looking much better this morning."

"Sheriff Wilson—Blaine . . ." she felt the blush stain her cheeks. "I...I'm sorry. I should've . . ." she trailed off.

He nodded but didn't reply.

Laura was still sitting on the porch when Blaine returned a few minutes later.

"You probably ought to take the day and rest up," he suggested, his expression still strained. He was watching her with that disturbingly intense gaze. And he hesitated before he spoke again. "From what Tom told me, Curry was aiming for you when he shot Glen. Do us all a favor and stay close to home."

She averted her gaze, but nodded.

Laura didn't look up as he pulled away. She walked into the kitchen to find Robey and Hattie sharing a second cup of coffee and talking about old times again. But Aunt Hattie got up then, claiming she had some laundry to do.

Laura poured herself another cup and sat down at the table with Robey. Her mother stared down into the dark liquid steaming in her cup, seemingly transfixed. Laura reached across the table and placed a hand over one of Robey's. She studied their matching prominent veins and crooked pinky fingers.

Robey looked up then with tears in her eyes. "Sheriff Wilson told me about the confession. Showed me the papers and asked if I wanted to read them. I told him no. I already know enough. I don't want the gory details to linger in my mind. I want to hold on to something of what he was to me back then, to the father he was to you. He loved you too much to let you grow up in the shadow of what he'd done." Robey spoke as if to offer some sliver of comfort in this reasoning.

"And I loved him too much not to honor his wish," she continued. "His sacrifice, such as it was . . . I loved *you* too much to put that burden on you. I guess it's why I would snap at you when you asked. Why I kept you at arm's length when you were going through the teen years and questioning everything."

Laura bit her lip and looked up at her mother.

Robey looked down then and sighed, "And I knew what was wrong with Lottie Edwards. That's why it scared me so when your daughter, Barbara, was born with Down Syndrome. Laura, I know it's no excuse for the distance and hard feelings, but I just didn't know how to tell you—any of it." Robey took her other hand and patted it on top of Laura's.

They sat that way quietly for several minutes. Only this time the silence felt . . . healing. The barriers they'd built between them were finally collapsing.

Laura spotted the photo albums on the end of the table then and motioned toward them. "Can you tell me who all these people are? And how in the heck we know them?" she asked with a wry smile as she pulled one open.

This time mother and daughter took a much needed walk down memory lane together. And Robey smiled, for real, as she pointed out the pictures and shared the stories.

CHAPTER 44

LAURA

Monday, October 18, 2010

They finally laid Glen Porter's body in the vacant grave that already bore his headstone. Tom promised to have the inscription changed to read *"Beloved Father,"* and to correct the death date.

Robey and Aunt Hattie were there. Tom and Elizabeth went to Beulah's to bring her and Loy out. The only service they had was graveside. And it was just a few words from Tom as he stood on crutches, unable to bear much weight on his bad leg.

The preacher didn't open a Bible. Instead he quoted an old song, *"Amazing grace, how sweet the sound that saved a wretch like me. 'Twas grace that taught my heart to fear and grace my fears relieved.* May God have mercy on your soul," he finished.

Then he laid a white rose on the coffin and placed his open palm on top. Quietly he added, "Goodbye, Daddy. I wish I could have done more to help you. But I always loved you."

Robey looked like she didn't dare speak or she'd burst. She laid a rose on top of Tom's.

When it was Laura's turn she added hers to the others, but she put both hands on the coffin and bent her head prayer-like. "Oh, Daddy," she whispered. "I know you loved me. I just wish—I wish things could've been different."

True to his word, Blaine Wilson was there. He went back to Tom Honeywell's with the family. Elizabeth had made lunch and they all sat down together. It was awkward at first. No one wanted to say anything that might be hurtful, so no one said anything at all.

Finally, the sheriff broke the silence as he made a fuss over the food and asked Elizabeth where she learned to cook so well, and told Tom what a lucky man he was. That got Tom started talking about how the two of them had met, and everyone seemed to visibly relax.

When Laura and Robey said their goodbyes, Blaine Wilson followed Laura out to her car. He carried the food Elizabeth had wrapped to send along for them. Robey lagged behind. On purpose, no doubt.

Blaine opened the back door of the Jeep and placed the food containers on the floor. He stood then and turned toward her. He was close, so close she had to look up sharply to see into his face. He stood there looking down at her for a moment.

Her breath got shallow and her face warmed.

"You'll be leaving soon?" he asked.

"I need to get back to work." *If I still have a job to go back to.* "We're leaving Wednesday morning around 8:00 a.m." Laura looked up at him as she finished speaking.

He nodded his head. Then he looked down at the ground before he spoke. "I was planning on going out there to comb those woods behind your Aunt Hattie's tomorrow morning. See if I can turn up anything. So don't be surprised if you see my car."

Laura wanted to explain why she'd gotten involved and apologize. She wanted to tell him about the dreams. She wanted to . . . but she simply said, "Okay."

Tuesday, October 19, 2010

Laura was up by 5:30 to shower and make herself presentable. She hoped to get another chance to talk to Blaine Wilson. And that was as far as she was willing to take the thought at the moment.

Breakfast was over and cleaned up already. Now Laura fretted between looking out the window and trying to pay attention to the conversation with the other two women. Robey gave her the high eyebrows and a grin.

At last the sheriff's SUV pulled in the driveway. Laura poured him a cup of coffee and carried it out onto the porch as Robey fussed over the last of the clean-up, insisting Hattie should sit down while she did.

Laura stepped out hesitantly, suddenly worried he'd think it was a little too forward of her to meet him at the door like this. But it was too late. She couldn't turn tail and run like a school girl.

So she watched him climb the steps to the porch and take the cup she reached out to him. There was something about this man's presence that was exhilarating and discomfiting at the same time.

He sat in the rocking chair quietly for several minutes as he studied his cup intently until he suddenly turned his head toward her and broke the silence.

"I suppose you'll be visiting your Aunt Hattie often?" he asked.

Laura smiled and nodded, "I hope to."

He clamped his lips shut and turned his attention back to the coffee. Laura watched him, wanting to speak up. Her heart pounded in her ears. She'd lost the moment.

"Just remember. Leave the search for murderers and villains to me." He stood and downed the rest of his coffee in one gulp then handed her the empty cup.

Robey came out onto the porch.

"You ladies have a safe trip home," he said, acknowledging Laura and her mother.

Blaine descended the steps with his hat still in his hand. He turned at the bottom and nodded to them both. But he looked directly at Laura—and finally smiled—as he gave her the two-fingered salute.

CHAPTER 45

CURRY

Monday, October 18, 2010

Fine sight to see. Laura Allen standing by the very gravestone he'd put there years ago himself. Crying like this wasn't all her fault in the first place. The way Curry saw it, if she hadn't found Lottie Edwards' body all them years ago none of this would've happened.

Women were evil. That's all there was to it. They used their eyes on a man the way Delilah used her scissors on Samson's hair. Drained the will right out of him, took his soul. Curry hated their eyes.

And now hers were leaking like she'd lost everything. "Hmmph, pluck 'em right out of her head. That's what'll fix it."

He caught movement to the side of the group by the grave. Loy stood there with his hand over his eyes, looking straight at Curry.

He slipped into the woods then and made his way back toward his new home.

ABOUT THE AUTHOR

Yvonne Schuchart holds a degree in Social Sciences and has worked with troubled youths in a residential program. She also worked as a freelance writer for the York Daily Record and ran a small horse farm for several years. Besides her love of reading and writing, she enjoys hiking, the outdoors, riding motorcycle and spending time with family. She lives in a tiny mill town in southcentral Pennsylvania.

 YvonneSchuchartAuthor

 @cinzims

 yvonne-schuchart.com

KEEP IN TOUCH

Be first to learn when the sequel is ready!
Sign up at yvonne-schuchart.com

Made in the USA
Middletown, DE
24 September 2016